"I told you he was wealthy," Nick said. "What did you think I meant?"

"I thought, you know, movie star wealthy, not Jeff Bezos wealthy," I snapped.

"I think you need to allow them to test your hair. We can find out, once and for all, if you're the child he's seeking. Miller has a hair sample from the baby and there was a sample taken from you when you were found. Those two match. All you need to prove is that you're the girl from the tower. I'd testify to that and so would other people." Jake looked at Nick, who nodded. "That won't hold up in court, though. Only the hair sample will do it. All the facts point to it, but there's an outside chance it isn't you." When I started to speak, he continued, overriding me. "A very slim outside chance. If it isn't, then you're off the hook and life goes back to normal."

"But what if I am?" I stood, anxious to move. "I can't be a billionaire, Jake. I'm not cut out to manage that kind of money." I paced in front of the fireplace, trying to sort out everything that was said.

Heir

by

J L Wilson

*Remembered Classics Romance
Series*

Heir

Cover Art by *Kim Mendoza*

The Wild Rose Press, Inc.
PO Box 708
Adams Basin, NY 14410-0708
Visit us at www.thewildrosepress.com

Publishing History
First Edition, 2023
Trade Paperback ISBN 978-1-5092-5142-1
Digital ISBN 978-1-5092-5143-8

Remembered Classics Romance Series
Published in the United States of America

Chapter 1

"I doubt if I'm the long-lost daughter of a millionaire." I ripped open the business-sized envelope and pulled out the sheaf of papers.

"You never know." My shop clerk/right-hand woman, Janice, watched while I skimmed the cover letter of the dense pile of legalese. Her sharp blue eyes regarded me over the top of her dime-store cheater glasses, bright green to match her sweater. Janice had glasses for every outfit. "For all you know, there may be a king or a queen somewhere, wishing their little princess could be returned to them."

I shot her a long-suffering look. I made the mistake once of telling Janice that I'd been an abandoned baby. It was a story far easier to believe than my true unusual upbringing. Now she looked for clues to my parentage in every scam and scheme that came my way. "This princess is just fine where she is."

"Please. Wouldn't you trade life in Centerville, Iowa, for the glitz and glamor of—" She snatched the envelope from my desk. "Portland, Oregon?" She dropped it back in my In Box, which held three bills to pay. "Okay, so it's not the Riviera or Monaco."

I skimmed the cover letter. Apparently a lawyer somewhere in Oregon had the notion that I was related to August Miller, a man who appeared to have a lot of disposable income to be spent looking for a lost child.

I tossed the letter on top of the other papers. "I'm fifty-five years old," I said. "It's a bit late in the game for anybody to be claiming me as a dependent." The door to my shop opened and two white-haired ladies entered, peering around. "Go now. Work your magic. They look like our kind of people."

Janice bustled out the door and into the main area of the shop. My office was tucked back in one corner of the two-story frame house that contained the Funky Fun Emporium. We specialized in unusual wares from local craftspeople. Jewelry, handbags made from recycled blue jeans, kitchen trivets and potholders, sweaters, and anything themed with the Fighting Bobcats, our local college mascot, had a place in our store. Each room of the house had a different flavor, with the living room reserved for football season, which was an extended four-month holiday in our college town. My apartment was upstairs, small but adequate for my needs.

I leaned back in my office chair and regarded the legal documents on my desk. Portland, Oregon was too close to my actual place of birth for my peace of mind. What were the odds that someone had tracked me down to this town smack in the middle of Iowa? My records were supposed to be sealed, and I had lived in anonymity for forty years, since I was found at age sixteen locked in that tower room.

What were the odds?

Janice poked her head in the door. "Do we have any more of the dish cozies for the microwave? I thought we had more in the cabinet but I can't find them."

I scooped up the legal papers and tucked them into the bottom rack of my desktop file system, that section designated *Someday*. "I'll see if I can find them. I think

Marlene dropped off a box yesterday." I left my office and the inheritance question behind, so I could focus on the more important task of restocking our shelves.

We were busy the rest of the day with pre-Christmas shoppers. Centerville, where my shop was located, had held an all-day open house on the past Sunday, which brought out a bunch of post-Thanksgiving Day shoppers. There was still a celebratory feeling three days later. Our town relied heavily on college visitors and other people attracted to its bucolic charm. We were equidistant from Des Moines, Iowa City, and Cedar Rapids, all major population centers for Iowa. We frequently got people seeking an unusual or unique gift.

I tallied the till at the end of the day and gave Janice the deposit for the bank, where she'd stop on her way home. "I hope this keeps up," I said. "I wonder if that advertisement in the *Des Moines Register* paid off."

"I'm sure it did," she said, pulling on her winter coat. "Four ladies today told me they saw it in Sunday's paper and came here to check it out for themselves." Her brown coat puffed up her already plump figure. Janice was my age, fifty-five, with artfully dyed brown hair and a beautiful complexion that spoke to her Norwegian heritage. She also had exactly the right personality for her job because she honestly enjoyed helping people find just the right thing among the hundreds of items in our store. Her helpful hints and willingness to take time with people, especially the elderly, endeared her to many of our clients.

"I'll look at doing the same for the other newspapers." I jotted a note, tucking it into my sweater pocket.

"It's not only good for us. They said they were

shopping at the bakery and the sewing center down the street." She pulled her gloves out of her pocket. "The Grimes house is up for sale. That's a prime location."

She was right. The house in question was on a northwest corner facing the town square. It had recently housed a boutique on the ground floor. The upstairs was rented out as an apartment. "I don't like Victorians," I said.

"It's a First-Tier house," she persisted. "Great location."

First Tier were those houses with businesses that opened directly onto the town square. Our store was in the Second Tier, behind the other houses on the south side of the square. There were plenty of signage and adequate sidewalks to get people to our spot, but she was right. A First-Tier house would be a far better location.

"I don't like Victorians," I repeated.

"Just think what we could do with the towers, though. Those turrets are so cool." She kept her eyes fixed on me while she spoke. I was hard-pressed to come up with a believable lie.

"Circular rooms are awkward," I said. "Besides, it's probably out of my price range." It probably wouldn't be. The settlement from the university years before meant I had a nice savings account. Not extravagant but comfortable.

Janice was like a dog with a bone once she got an idea in her head. I jotted another note and tore it off the *Jessa Rampion* notepad sent to me by some charity. "I'll call the Realtor," I said. "I suppose we can take a tour sometime."

She beamed at me. "We deserve to be First Tier. Our stock is as good as that in Carla's Clothing and certainly better than Hank's Hobbies." She picked up her bulging handbag and left by the back door, leaving me to lock up in front.

I did just that, walking around and turning off lights and flipping the *Open* sign to *Closed.* The sidewalk separating our house from the First-Tier house in front of us had a light dusting of snow. It applied a pristine glow to the grayish mound piled from a storm last week. We had a Christmas-y appearance, something that really helped boost shoppers and sales.

I went back to my office and turned off my desk lamp. The envelope caught my eye where it sat, half in and half out of the bottom bin. I took it with me while I went to the back and turned off lights there. I went upstairs to my apartment, the wooden steps creaking and groaning while I went.

I emerged on the second floor, my living room on the right and my bedroom on the left. Straight ahead was the bathroom, complete with claw-foot tub and old free-standing sink. I went into the living room to the window overlooking the town square, seen through the gap between the two First-Tier houses in front of me.

People walked across the open space, going to parked cars. Most stores were open on Monday and Thursday evenings during the holiday shopping season so there were few people out and about on this Wednesday night. I dropped the bulky envelope on a chair and went into my kitchen through the wide entryway between that room and the living room. I fixed a pre-dinner drink then returned to sink into my favorite armchair.

I dumped out all the legal papers on my ottoman and read through the cover letter again. It certainly appeared legit. I browsed through some of the other documents, but it was mainly composed of dense legalese. I tossed it back on the ottoman and considered my options. Was this really a possible key to my birth parents and my background?

I had no memory of them because I had been given away when I was just a baby. Over the years, I had been curious, of course, but I never sought any information. For the first dozen years or so, I assumed that my captor, Dr. Thell, was my parent. As my knowledge of the world expanded, I began to question that notion. That's when she told me that my mother was a junkie and my father was a homeless vagrant. I had no reason to doubt her. She was my sole contact with The Other World, the world outside my tower.

Was this an opportunity to find out more about my family? How did anyone find me? I had a made-up name, my records were sealed, and I had been spirited away from Portland with no one the wiser that I was gone. I was a brief media star, and then I faded, the same way all pop culture stars fade.

I knew one person who might be able to help. I picked up my cell phone from its charging cradle and dialed my aunt Wil. She wasn't really my aunt, but she had a major impact on my life when I was freed from my tower prison. Wilhelmina Brothers had been the court-appointed attorney charged with guarding my interests. She and her husband Jake became surrogate family for me during that bewildering introduction to the world almost forty years ago. She'd become a judge several years earlier, and we still stayed in touch.

Jake answered the phone. "Hey, Punzi, how are you?" he asked.

I grinned at his use of that nickname. He used to tease me and call me Rapunzel because I had been held prisoner in a tower. When I was rescued, I had long white-blonde hair reaching almost to my knees. Jake was a small, wiry guy whose outdoorsy appearance had served him well when he was a defense attorney.

"I'm doing fine, Jake. I had a question for you or Wil if you have time."

"Nothing but time now that I'm retired. What's the deal?"

"I got some information in the mail. A guy apparently is looking for his long-lost daughter. He thinks I might be her."

There was a long pause. I could imagine Jake, his gray-and-white hair tumbling over his forehead when he ran his hand through his curls. That was Jake's normal response in regular conversation. In the courtroom he was known as The Statue, unmoving and calm. "Hold on. Let me get Wil. Maybe she picked up some gossip down at the courthouse."

Before I could stop him, the line went quiet. That was an odd response, I decided. I hadn't mentioned where the papers came from, never implying that it was in their neck of the woods. For all he knew, it might have been someone in Iowa seeking me out.

Maybe it was because Wil had been my court-appointed guardian. If any inquiries about me came in, they should technically go through Wil first. I know she had set up alerts for my records, so she'd be notified if anyone was poking around.

"Punzi, how are you doing? It's been a while since we talked." Wil's cheerful, bubbly voice sounded just like she looked—youthful despite white hair, slender and willowy, and full of energy. She was such a contrast to Jake with her urban sophistication. They made an odd couple, but a marvelous one.

"I know. Where does the time go? I feel like it's been just a few weeks and it's been what? A year or more?"

"How's the store doing?"

"Good. I have no complaints about it or my choice of home. I enjoy it there."

"I'm so glad to hear it. If anyone deserves a happy ending, it's you. How can I help you? Jake mumbled something about family?"

That was the Wil I knew and loved. Always down to business as quickly as possible. I described the packet of material I received. "Someone named August Miller is looking for his child, I guess. What I wonder about is why I got the information."

"Let me look into it," she said immediately. "Give me the name of the attorney and their contact information."

I was relieved. There was nothing like having a judge call you and ask about your business practices to make any attorney sit up and take notice. She assured me that she'd do some research and get back to me with results. We chatted a bit longer, then we ended the call. I promptly put it all out of my mind and refocused on getting ready for the Christmas shopping rush.

It was a week later that the shop bell rang and a man walked into the store. Janice, alert to a possible customer, hurried to the front to greet him. He towered over her, seeming to fill the small foyer at the front. He had to be at least six-and-a-half feet tall and was broad-shouldered and, well, big. His opened winter coat showed a red Vneck sweater over a white shirt and striped necktie. He wore dark blue jeans and heavy boots, a good choice for the cold winter day.

"Can I help you?" Janice stepped back to look up at him properly.

He glanced around the shop. I had a good view of him because I was behind a display of amusing handmade signs with phrases like *I'm not retired, I'm just getting started* and *Would you like some cheese with that whine?* He was handsome in an understated sort of way, his thick, brown-gold hair cut short to frame his oval face. His neatly trimmed beard highlighted a rather prominent chin, and his eyes seemed very sharp while he examined my store.

"I'd like to speak with Jessa Rampion," he said in a low voice.

"May I say who's asking?" Janice smiled brightly at him, using her best executive assistant voice.

He pulled a card from his coat pocket and handed it to her. "Give that to her if you would. I think she'll want to talk to me."

Janice glanced at the business card. "Just browse around a bit. I'll see if she has time to chat with you." She gestured to a display of mittens made from discarded sweaters. "It's never too early to get your Christmas shopping done." She wheeled about and headed for the back of the store.

I scurried out of my hiding place and met her at the door to my office. "There's a guy up front who—" she said.

"Yeah, I heard." I studied the card she handed me. *Wilhelmina Brothers, District Judge* was imprinted on it, with Aunt Wil's contact information underneath the name and title. I turned it over. *You need to talk to him* was written in Wil's angular, precise handwriting.

"Do you know him?" Janice asked. "He's a big one, isn't he? Look how tall he is."

I peered around her. The man had moved farther into the shop and now dwarfed a display of handbags. Our store catered more to a female shopper, but he appeared perfectly at ease among the doilies, crocheted tea cozies, and purses. "I don't know him, but my aunt vouches for him." I dropped the card on the desk and left the office, Janice trailing behind me.

"I'll hang around just in case," she offered.

"Just in case of what?" I don't know why I scoffed. I should have been grateful for her concern. For some reason those few words written on a business card set my nerves on edge. "I'll be fine." I made my way through the crowded aisles of the store to the stranger.

He turned when he heard us coming, a faint smile creasing his beard. "Miss Rampion?"

I extended my hand. "I'm Jessa Rampion. How can I help you?"

"I'm Nick Kingson. Wil Brothers asked me to get in touch with you." His handshake was cool and firm as was the gaze that swept me from head to toe.

"Come into my office." I turned to lead the way and almost ran over Janice, who blocked my path. "It's okay," I said softly.

"I'll be right out here," she replied. "In case you need me."

I nodded. "Good." It was futile to argue with her, I knew. Janice had a proprietary interest in me and the shop. She would protect both as much as possible.

I went into the office, and Kingson came in behind

me, taking the wooden guest chair in front of my desk. It appeared almost comically small contrasted with his bulk and the heavy winter coat he wore. "How can I help you?" I touched the business card on the desk blotter.

"It's about the information that was sent to you." He propped his right ankle on his left knee, his glance going around the room quickly.

"What about it?"

"We think it's legitimate. We believe it is your parents trying to get in touch with you."

I regarded him warily. "Why did Wil decide to send you? Why didn't she just call me?"

"I used to work with Jake before he retired. I was retired and was kind of at loose ends. I did some investigative work for him."

That made sense, I suppose. Jake had been a defense attorney. I knew he sometimes had cases that required a lot of manpower. "Well, thanks, I guess. But you didn't need to waste the time. I don't know if I want to get involved in anything with my so-called parents."

"Wil said you might feel that way. She thought it was best that you discuss it with someone rather than try to handle it all long distance." He looked away, not meeting my eyes. "She asked me to come because I know you."

"What?" Of all the things he might have said, I didn't expect that. "Where do I know you from? I don't recognize you."

"I was there that day." His voice was soft and low. Now his eyes were fixed on me from under his eyelashes.

That's when I realized I recognized his eyes. One eye was blue and the other a startling green. I flopped back in my chair, memory flooding me. It had been almost forty years, but the sensations were burned into my brain. The smell of blood. The faded carpet where I lay, unable to move. Voices above me, shouting. The sticky feeling of whatever-it-was between my legs when I sprawled on the floor. Sunlight flickering over my face and making patterns on my eyelids. His face, above me, concern in those odd-colored eyes.

And yet it wasn't him. Where was the sweet, innocent young police officer, his face so smooth and youthful? Where was the boy-man who held me while I wept?

"I don't know you." My voice was trembling and so were my hands.

"I was the police officer who was on the scene."

On the scene. What a prosaic way to say *at the place where you almost bled to death because of a miscarriage.* "I don't recognize you," I repeated stupidly.

"It's been a long time." His eyes seemed to glow with intensity. Then his face relaxed and his gaze softened.

It was him. I remembered him kneeling on the rug next to me, his hand under my head to lift me so he could stare into my face. He had such baby smooth skin then, the skin of a young man near my own age, sixteen then. "You were so young," I whispered. "I didn't believe you were with the police."

"I was twenty. Just starting with the department." He looked around my office, nodding at the picture of Jake, Wil, and me at a picnic when I had just gotten out of the hospital. "Judge Brothers wasn't sure if you'd remember me."

I didn't remember him specifically, but more the

way he treated me. He had lifted me in his arms, carrying me down the stairs in the tower. The door at the bottom was open to the outside walled garden, but he didn't go through it. He went through the other door, the one that led to The Outside. We passed through it and for the first time in my sixteen years, I was near a vehicle, the squad car sitting at the curb.

I was barely conscious from loss of blood. The other policeman there looked ready to protest when the young officer—this man in front of me, Nick—put me in the back seat and climbed in with me. "Drive," Nick shouted and the other man got behind the wheel.

I became aware of movement, of Nick awkwardly supporting me, of a jacket or something being pressed against my crotch. Then it was darkness. I woke in a hospital. The first person I saw was Wilhelmina, sitting by my bed, her head bent while she studied the papers in her lap.

I never saw the young policeman again except for a glimpse of him in the courthouse during the trial. That was months later. I looked back over my shoulder and saw him gazing at me. I wasn't sure how to interpret what I saw in that look. I had never had a chance to ask him.

Until now. Now his face was etched with experience, lines around his mouth and eyes. And his eyes were no longer hopeful and young. These were the eyes of a man who had seen brutality, had seen hatred and injustice and pain. This was no longer that young and idealistic police officer.

"What is this all about?" I asked. "Why would you come all the way to Iowa? I don't understand."

"I'm retired and I had nothing better to do. When

Wil asked me to help, I was glad to do it." The answer came too quickly and was too well rehearsed. I tapped an edge of the business card against the open software catalog on my desk. I'd been researching new inventory systems with a thought about upgrading next year if I could squeeze it out of my budget. "Judge Brothers felt it would be better if I could explain it to you in person."

"Explain what? That someone thinks I might be related to him? How did they find me? I was promised anonymity."

"The family is quite wealthy. It's possible they paid someone to get the information."

"How could they prove anything after all these years?" I tugged out the legal papers from the bottom file drawer on my desk and stared at them.

"We need a hair sample for DNA. They took a hair sample years ago when you were found. It matched the sample of the baby's hair that the parents had from their child. They need to confirm that you are who you say you are."

"You know as well as I do that I can't prove anything," I snapped. "I have a made-up name and history. I can't prove who I am."

"I'm sorry. I didn't explain that well. Mr. Miller is already sure that the girl in the tower is his daughter because the hair sample taken then matches the hair sample he has from the baby. All we need to do is prove to him that you are the girl in the tower. They want a sample of your hair to compare it to the hair sample taken when you were rescued."

I glanced at the open doorway. Janice was hovering outside, ostensibly straightening a rack of Bobcat-themed scarves. I rolled my eyes, knowing I had a Life

Story to tell in my near future. "Why should I care?" I countered. "My parents traded me for heroin."

"He's ill and he wants to make amends. It's important to him that you have a share of your mother's estate."

Something in his wording made me pause. "Wait a minute. You said him. I thought both parents were alive."

He smiled faintly. "I'm not telling this very well, am I? Your mother came from a very wealthy family who had lumber and mining interests in the Pacific Northwest. She ran away from home at a young age, met your father, and they lived what I guess you'd call a hippie lifestyle. After she gave birth, she became addicted to drugs. Six months after you were born, they gave you up, but your father never forgot about you."

"Gave me up?" I smiled mirthlessly. "They sold me."

He winced. "Your mother died of an overdose a month after they surrendered you. Your father later remarried. You have a stepsister, stepbrother, and a stepmother. Your father is truly remorseful about what happened."

"You mean selling me to a woman who used me as an experiment for sixteen years?" I didn't try to keep the bitterness out of my voice.

"I know how it must seem. Too little, too late."

I tapped the papers on my desk. "It's more like he's trying to buy my love. How much are we talking about? You said he wanted me to have a share of my mother's estate."

"He wants you to have her entire estate. It's worth millions. He inherited it when she died, and it's become entwined with his estate. But he's kept records and he wants you to have all of hers."

I gaped at him. "What?"

"Holy crap," I heard a faint voice exclaim from the depths of the shop.

"That's why Judge Brothers wanted me to speak with you. This isn't a trivial amount. You'll be an heiress once your identity is proven. She felt it might be wise if someone is with you because it's possible there might be some contention about your inheritance."

"Contention?"

"Your stepmother is understandably concerned that your father's estate might go to someone other than her or her children."

"Are you saying I might be in danger?" I countered.

"What?" that voice from the shop said again.

Kingson glanced over his shoulder. "No, nothing like that. It's just that if word gets out about this, you may acquire some unwanted publicity. Judge Brothers thought I might be able to help run interference for you." He smiled wryly. "So to speak."

I drummed my fingers on the desk. "I didn't ask to be an heiress and I didn't ask for his interest. He's trying to buy my love."

"Not your love." Kingson's eyes caught and held mine. "Your forgiveness."

I stared down at the business card. Anywhere but at him. "I'll consider it," I said grudgingly.

"Thank you. That's really all we ask."

"We?"

"Judge Brothers and me."

"Why do you care?"

That seemed to fluster him. He stood, pulling his coat up to settle on his broad shoulders. "It's the right thing to do, I guess. I'm staying at the Garden View Hotel across the square. Could we go out for dinner tonight? I promise I won't pressure you about it," he said quickly when he saw me hesitate.

I glanced at the door. Janice was in the shadows, frowning at me and nodding vigorously. "All right."

"Good. Can we meet at five-thirty in the hotel lobby? Perhaps we can eat in the dining room there or somewhere else if you'd prefer."

The Garden View had one of the better restaurants in town. "That's fine. You may want to stop at the desk and get a reservation. It's often booked."

He nodded. "I'll do that. Thank you, Miss Rampion." He turned to the door, almost running over Janice, who darted out of the way. She escorted him to the front, chatting brightly while she walked.

A minute later she appeared in my office doorway again. "Okay. Spill the beans. What was that all about?" She settled in the guest chair recently vacated by Nick Kingson.

I sighed. "You probably heard about me. It was in all the news. After my story broke, laws were changed so young mothers could find a safe place for unwanted babies."

She frowned, eyebrows drawn together in thought. "What do you mean?"

"It was forty years ago." I paused, letting her do the math in her head. She nodded slowly. "I was kept a prisoner in a Victorian house from the time I was born until I was almost seventeen years old."

Her mouth opened in an O of surprise. "You're her. You're the girl in the tower."

Chapter 2

"So it's all true?" Janice asked. "The millionaire's daughter and all that?" She pointed to the pile of papers on my desk.

"Maybe," I said.

"You were really kept in a tower, locked away from everybody?"

I nodded. "Everyone except Professor Thell. She raised me."

"Raised you? I thought she kept you captive. I think I read about you in a social psychology class when I was in college," she said. "They called you Patient J or something like that, right?"

"My identity was protected. Psychologists had a field day when I was found. I had been traded for heroin to a psychology professor who used me as her own private experiment. I had no contact with the outside world except what I could see out my window and what I experienced in a walled garden outside the house."

"There are all kinds of case studies and reports and—"

"And Wikipedia entries." I nodded. "I was one of the lucky ones. I wasn't abused. Not really."

"But you were in a tower room with no contact with the world." Janice's well-defined eyebrows drew together in confusion. "That's abuse, isn't it?"

I shook my head. "It was all normal to me. I didn't

question it. Why should I? It was all I knew."

"But what about TV and movies and radio and all that?"

"I didn't see a TV until I was seventeen years old. It's hard for people to understand. I had books. All kinds of books. I read the encyclopedia and the dictionary and all kinds of textbooks. I wasn't given any fiction, though. Dr. Thell was trying to gauge what the lack of social and peer contact would do to a child." I smiled faintly. "She talked to me a lot and took tons of notes. Social psychologists found a gold mine when they found me."

"They talked about that in class. How do we judge reality? You thought that was all real. Everybody has their own reality." She frowned. "It was weird. I never considered that before. But wait a minute. Peer contact? You mean you never saw any other kids?"

"I did sometimes from the window." I looked away from her perceptive gaze. "That's how I met Bobby. He saw me one day when I was out in the walled garden. He came back when Dr. Thell was teaching a class. One thing led to another and…" I shrugged.

"Oh, I remember now, reading about that. There was a fight, wasn't there? You were injured? The guy was hurt, too, right?"

I shook my head. I didn't dare tell her the details. It was horribly messy and too painful, even after all those years. Bobby Reagan had used me, a naïve, innocent child-like girl-woman. When Dr. Thell found out, she was livid. She lay in wait for Bobby and almost killed him when she stabbed him with a pair of scissors. Then she stabbed me in the abdomen, a wound that later festered and almost killed me.

That's how Nick Kingson found me, lying on the

rug. Bobby had fled. I didn't know what had happened to him for months because I was kept isolated in the hospital, gradually taught about the world around me and reintroduced to it carefully with Wil and Jake to guide me. "I had to give a statement, but it was in chambers so I didn't know what happened to anyone until long after it was over." The glib lie came easily.

"How did you end up in the middle of Iowa?"

I was relieved that she posed a prosaic question. My whole past history with Bobby Reagan and Dr. Thell was so unbelievable to anyone raised in conventional society. "I was given a settlement by the university where Dr. Thell taught. Wil made sure of that. I think they were worried about publicity. Wil and Jake found me a therapist who helped me understand this brave new world that I was thrust into." I raised my hands to encompass the shop and all it contained. "I attended a small college, graduated with a degree in business administration. I gradually got the experience I needed to fit in by working at various companies. I managed one gift shop for a friend and decided I enjoyed it. Jake had a cousin who lived here in town. She's the one who suggested I move out here."

"Wow. What a terrible experience." Janice's sympathy was reflected in her sad blue eyes.

"It's hard to explain. I suppose to others it was horrible, but like I said, to me, it was all normal. What was hard was when I discovered the rest of the world existed. That was a struggle, believe me." I rested my hand on the stack of papers. "But that was almost forty years ago. I've had a lot of time to put it all behind me."

"Why did your aunt—Wil—why did she send that guy out? Why didn't she just call?"

Apparently Janice missed that part of the conversation. "I think she thought it would have more weight if someone presented it all in person."

"What are you going to do?"

I glanced past her to the clock. "I'm going to read through all this again, then I guess I'll meet him for dinner."

"That makes sense. After all, he came all this way. And tonight's prime-rib night at the Garden View. You know they have the best prime rib around."

"Well, since this is Iowa, I guess that's saying a lot."

She grinned. "You know what they say. It isn't fresh unless it was walking around this morning."

I wrinkled my nose at the thought. "It's comments like that which make me consider becoming a vegetarian."

"And forgo the pleasure of the Garden View prime rib? No way." Janice stood. "Why don't you go on and get ready for your date. I'll handle closing up."

I gathered up the papers and stuffed them all back into the envelope. "I'll take you up on that offer. Thanks. And thanks for having my back earlier. I appreciate it."

"Us girls have to stick together. No way am I leaving you with a strange man alone. Now go and get ready. Make sure to drive to the restaurant. I don't want you walking across the town square at night alone."

I smiled at her concern. "Thanks for the advice." I followed her out of my office, closing the door behind me. I went to the stairs, hidden from the public by a door marked Employees Only. I opened it and went up, going to the front window to peer through the gap between the Tier One houses. I could see the Garden View Hotel across the square. What an odd turn of events. Millions of dollars? Impossible.

Or was it? Kingson's explanation seemed almost reasonable. I considered calling Wil, but she was probably still in court given the time difference with the west coast. I decided to call her when I got home from dinner.

I heard the door downstairs close. That odd silence settling over the house told me the shop was closed. I went into my bedroom and reviewed my clothing options. I settled on black jeans and a Christmas-themed sweater made by one of the craftsmen I featured in the shop. It had a light snowy background with small embroidered snow-covered trees on it, with one tree festooned with small "lights." I seldom had anywhere fancy to wear it so I was happy to pull it out and find that it still fit.

My pale white-blonde hair was easily styled into an upswept, poofy bun. I never grew it out so long again after Dr. Thell attacked me. She had grabbed me by my braid and shaken me so hard that I fell against a table, my head smacking into the floor. When I tried to defend Bobby, Dr. Thell turned on me and used the scissors to slash at me. She kicked me when I tried to get away. I think the trauma of having her use my hair to restrain me had somehow convinced me to never allow it to grow out again. I kept it at a bit past shoulder length and almost always wore it twisted into a French roll at the back.

Despite what I told Janice, I decided to walk to the restaurant. Centerville was a quiet little town, and I felt perfectly safe on foot. The town square held a gazebo and had crisscrossing sidewalks. I wore my one pair of somewhat fashionable boots, which would be sufficient for a short walk. I decided to take the long way and walk around the square, passing the Victorian house for sale.

I paused to view it in the dusky light. It was an attractive building, painted a pale blue with dark blue shutters. But I couldn't repress the coldness I felt when I viewed the two large turrets on the second floor. I had spent years of my early life in a similar circular room. I wasn't sure I wanted to envision more years in my later life in such a place. I continued walking, tucking the thought away to be considered another day.

The Garden View Hotel occupied two-thirds of the block adjacent to the Victorian house. It was an old-fashioned three-story structure of limestone with arched windows that glowed with light in the dusk. It was more than one hundred years old but had been renovated so it was modern underneath its Art Deco façade.

I entered the restaurant through the street-side door, not through the lobby. The hostess at the doorway podium smiled brightly at me. I spied Nick Kingson seated at the ornate wooden bar behind the hostess in the dimly lit cocktail lounge. I passed her and headed for him, pausing to hand my coat to the woman in the coat-check cubicle.

I made my way around the people relaxing over their drinks. The place had a subdued old-world air like some far-off meeting place in Europe. Or so I imagined. I had never traveled overseas and just formed my opinions based on books I read. But the Garden View's quiet, genteel atmosphere always made me feel like I was stepping through a door in France or maybe Italy.

I walked around the horseshoe-shaped bar. When I rounded the curve, I saw Kingson watching me. He wore a denim sport coat over a light blue shirt with dark jeans. The colors contrasted with the sandy gray of his hair. I couldn't interpret the look I saw. For an instant he looked regretful, as though he felt sorry for me. Then that look was replaced by one of sadness. He smiled tentatively and slipped off his barstool when I approached.

"I made a reservation for six-fifteen, and I was lucky to get it," he said when I got to him. "You weren't kidding. This is a busy place."

"It's the nicest place in town. Everyone comes here when they have something to celebrate."

He pulled out the barstool next to his. "I saved you a seat."

I used the bar rail to give me the boost I needed to get into the seat. "See what I mean?" I peered past him.

He turned to look. A boy stood in the doorway by the hostess table, looking gawky and ill-at-ease in his obviously store-bought suit. A girl was with him dressed in a frothy dress with dark lace at the collar and cuffs and high heels that seemed precarious to me.

Kingson shook his head. "Man, I remember those awkward first dates. It takes all the courage you can muster to ask somebody out. When they accept, you panic."

I smiled even though I had no idea of what he meant. I didn't have such awkward first dates when I was growing up.

He seemed to realize what he said because his cheeks darkened. "I'm sorry," he stammered. "I keep forgetting you didn't have—" He stopped, his cheeks reddening even more.

"A normal life?" I nodded to the bartender, a slender girl with upswept brown hair. "A glass of pinot grigio," I said.

"I guess that's what I meant. Although what's

normal anymore?"

"Isn't that the truth? The world seems mad sometimes. Election fraud, last year's pandemic, weather woes. I wonder sometimes if we aren't in the End Times." I looked at the relaxed people gathered in the cozy space. "It's easy to forget there's a world out there, isn't it?"

"It's still there, somewhere." He smiled wryly. "Sometimes it can catch up to you."

"Tell me about yourself," I said. "How long were you a police officer?" I took the glass of wine the bartender set down and sipped. "Where did you grow up?"

"I grew up in Rampian. My father was a police officer there."

"So you followed in his footsteps?"

"I guess you could say that. He died when I was four years old. He was shot during a burglary investigation."

"That's terrible," I said. "I'm sorry."

"I don't remember much about him. My mother remarried when I was twelve. I got a stepfather and a stepbrother in that deal."

From his tone of voice, it sounded like it wasn't a deal that made him happy. "And then you decided to go into your father's profession. How did your stepfather feel about that?"

"I don't think he cared. He had his own son to inherit his business. No, he didn't care as long as my profession didn't interfere with his."

"What do you mean?"

The hostess approached. "Your table is ready, sir."

We took our drinks and followed her to a small, two-person table near the windows overlooking the town square. Snow was falling, just enough to soften the outlines of the benches in the square. It also softened the town statue of a Native American woman credited with saving pioneer settlers during a terrible snowstorm.

We spent a few minutes examining the menu, then I set mine aside. "I suppose I should thank your mother. After all, it's because of her I have a name."

Kingson looked at me over the top of his menu. "I wasn't sure if you remembered that."

"It's hard to forget. They didn't want to admit me to the hospital unless I had a name."

"It wasn't that they wouldn't admit you. They just didn't have an easy way to process you, especially because you had no identification."

"All my life I was called Girl. I knew I lived in Rampian because I saw that on letters that came to the house now and then. But I didn't have a first name. You told them my name was Jessa and the rest is history."

"I suppose we could have used Jane Doe." He set his menu down and stared into his cocktail glass. "You weren't just a Jane Doe, though. I'll never forget it. You were so beautiful. So young. I couldn't believe that someone would hurt you like that." He smiled faintly. "I was young myself."

"I had no idea that Bobby was the son of a rich man, someone so well respected in town. I was stupid about things like that."

"I was stupid, too. I couldn't believe that anyone could be so callous and cruel. It was a shocking introduction to police life."

"And yet you stayed in the business," I said. "You must have liked helping people."

"It got harder and harder while time went on. There

are so many rules that seemed to get in the way of helping."

He sounded slightly depressed or reflective. I was glad when the waitress came and took our order and I could change the subject. "You said you were born in Rampian. Did you stay there for your entire police career?"

He seemed relieved to change the subject. I found out that he had moved several times, to Portland, San Francisco, and finally returning to the small town when his mother became elderly and needed care. He didn't mention his stepfather or stepbrother. I didn't ask because that seemed to be a prickly topic. He was married briefly and amicably divorced with no children. "Since I left the force, I do some work for Wil and some other folks in the legal business now and then. Otherwise I just putter around my workshop, play bad golf, and work cold case files from around the country."

"Really? That's interesting. How did you get involved with that?"

He fiddled with his silverware, not meeting my gaze. "I wanted to help families who have waited so long for answers. Imagine how cruel it must be to never know what happened to a loved one. Even if you find out definitely that the lost person is dead, at least you have that knowledge."

"I suppose you're right. How does that work? Do you go through all the files or something? Look for new clues?"

"Sometimes all it takes is another set of eyes to review all the evidence. When a detective works on a case, it can become familiar. It's easy to miss that tiny little bit of something that might make or break the case."

"Tiny bit of something?" I smiled.

"It could be just a phrase in an interview or maybe a matchbook out of place. Or a victim with fingernail polish that wasn't a color she usually wore." He finished his cocktail and moved the empty glass to one side, staring out at the bucolic scene. "Just a tiny bit of something."

"Can you tell me about some of the cases? Is that why Wil asked you to talk to me? Because I'm a cold case?"

His gaze snapped to me. "I never thought of it that way," he said. "I suppose you are."

"What do you think is the tiny bit of something that might prove my case, one way or the other?" I touched my head. "My hair?"

"It's such an unusual color. And hair DNA can be useful to prove maternity."

"Maternity? I thought it had, well, DNA. You know, the whole genetic thing."

"Not really. If hair is torn away from the scalp and still has a follicle, it can be seventy-five percent accurate to prove a person's identity. But cut hair can be used for a mitochondrial DNA test. That shows if two people share the same maternal line."

"I had no idea there was such a science to it." I moved to one side when the waitress brought our salads.

"Television makes it seem like every hair that's found is useful, but that's not always the case." He studied me in the low light of the restaurant. "Your hair would prove that you're related to your mother because we have her mitochondrial DNA test results and the results from the baby they gave away for adoption."

"Adoption?" I sprinkled salt on my salad. "You

28

should just say 'gave away.' "

"The way your father—your supposed father—talks, he thought it would be temporary. He knew he had to get his wife treatment for her addiction. They couldn't raise a child with her in that condition."

I wasn't going to argue with him. I suppose I sounded bitter about my odd life, but I really wasn't. After all, like I told Janice, as far as I was concerned, that was normal. I had nothing to compare it to. No, the past could stay in the past.

Dinner passed with Kingson asking me questions about my business. That led to some talk about how I got started with the local craftsmen and my own meager attempts at jewelry making and yard art created with recycled items.

We finished with coffee and cheesecake. "We shouldn't linger too long," I said, leaning over the table to speak to Kingson. "This restaurant is always busy, so I'll bet somebody's waiting for our seats."

He took my hint and we left the table soon after. I insisted on paying my share of the bill. Kingson didn't protest too vigorously, something I appreciated. "Can I see you to your car?" he asked when we paused by the coat check desk to get my coat.

"I walked." I slipped into the coat he held for me. "It's just a couple of blocks away." I looked through the glass door. "Looks like the snow has stopped."

"Let me get my coat and I'll walk you home."

"No, you don't have to, it's so close."

"I insist, and I won't take no for an answer. I'll be back in a second." He hurried across the lobby, heading for the stairs.

I considered just walking home without him, but that

seemed rude, so I waited, standing near the revolving front door and watching cars drive by. The evening had a soft look with a haze in the air and all the fresh snow. I felt almost as hazy, relaxed from a good dinner, quiet conversation, and two glasses of wine.

Kingson strode through the lobby, pulling on his long winter coat. It wrapped around his legs when he tugged it closed. For an instant I was reminded of a cowboy wearing his duster. I expected to see him settle a ten-gallon hat on his head. The thought made me smile and he regarded me quizzically. "Is something funny?"

"No. It's just such a pretty night." I pushed open the lobby door, and we stepped out into the chilly evening. "I like snowfalls."

He pulled his coat collar higher. "I've never lived anywhere that got really cold."

"You should try Minnesota. I lived there for a few years. Now that's cold." We crossed the street and walked through the square, lit by old-fashioned hanging streetlamps that cast a warm glow. "Iowa has cold and snowy winters, but they aren't as long as Minnesota's. We usually have spring a week or two earlier, and our snow doesn't usually start until November. In Minnesota, you might be surprised in October by a sudden snow."

We left the square and crossed the street to the sidewalk in front of the First-Tier stores on my side of the street. When we passed between buildings, I dug into my coat pocket for my keys, tucked there with the small wallet that held my cash and credit cards. While I was pulling out the keys, a flash of light caught my attention. It was one of those odd glimpses that made me look twice at the sidewalk leading around my store to the parking lot in back.

Something was out of place. I quickened my pace and was almost to the door when Kingson pulled me to a stop. "What's wrong?"

"I'm not sure. Something doesn't look right."

He gently moved me behind him. "Let me check it. Give me your key." I hesitated then put it in his hand. "Wait here."

Before I could protest, he was gone, striding to the door and peering inside. I followed more slowly, watching him try the door then inserting the key. "The lights are on the right," I said softly. "Just inside the doorway."

He opened the old wooden door and fumbled for the light switch. I looked around outside, noting my previous footprints that had been partially filled in by the snow. Other footprints led around the side of the building, also filled in. Those might be Janice's, although she usually left by the back door, which was nearer to the parking lot.

I followed Nick into the store, glancing quickly around the room. "How does it look to you?" he asked, blocking me from moving any farther.

I peered down at the sisal rug, stretching out into the store. It and the one on the front porch collected most of the debris brought in by customers. Janice shook out both rugs every night before closing up. It seemed dry. "I must be imagining things."

"Always trust your first instinct. If it's okay with you, I'll check around."

"Sure." I was relieved he said it. I was accustomed to managing most things on my own, but a potential thief was out of my league. I kept him in sight while he walked through the store, peeking into each separate alcove while he went. There was something in the way he moved that told me this was second nature for him, this watchful alertness that was like a sixth sense.

He completed a circuit of the store, and I met him at the stairs leading up to my apartment.

"Do you want to check upstairs?" I asked.

He nodded. "That makes sense, if you don't mind."

I unlocked the door and made a move to the steps, but he once again put his hand on my arm. "Let me go first." He brushed past me and started upward.

I always left a light on when I was gone, so the stairwell and living room were easy to navigate. He paused at the top of the stairs then turned to the left, opening the door to my bedroom. I flipped on the overhead light and he went in, checking the closet then leaving and going to the bathroom across the hall. "What's this?" he asked, pointing to the door at the end of the hallway.

"A storage closet."

He stared down at the floor, examining it. I realized he'd been doing that during his entire examination. When he opened the door, I held my breath, wondering if someone would leap out from among my Halloween decorations.

The phone ringing in the living room made me jump about a foot. I lost my balance, bumping into Nick. "Sorry," I muttered, righting myself and heading for the living room.

He went past the doorway and into the kitchen while I checked the display on the phone. *Wil Office.* "Hi, Wil. You're calling late." I watched Nick go through the kitchen to look at the fire escape outside the big south window.

"Hi, Punzi. I had some business to wrap up and wanted to talk to you before I headed for home. Did Nick Kingson get there and talk to you?"

"Yes, he's here with me now." I saw Nick open the window and lean over to check outside. I spied the legal papers still spread out on the hassock and moved to tidy them.

"Good. I wanted you to know how serious this is. Nick is good people. Make sure to take his advice."

"Advice?" I wedged the phone against my shoulder while I tried to corral the papers. "Advice about what?"

"You know, any advice he has about travel and meeting with the client."

"I don't have any plans to travel anywhere," I said. "Why would I?"

"Didn't he explain—wait a minute." Her voice faded. I got the impression she had lowered her phone.

Nick came back to stand in the doorway, hands in his coat pockets. "Everything looks good," he said softly.

"Thanks for checking." I dropped the file on the hassock and shifted the phone to my other hand. "It's Wil on the phone."

"Can I talk to her?"

I tuned him out when I heard Wil's loud voice in the receiver. "Get out. You have no business being here. How did you get in? The guards should have stopped you. If you don't leave I'll call them."

"Is everything okay, Wil?" I demanded.

"What is it? What's wrong?" Nick asked.

I shook my head. "It sounds like she's in trouble." I pressed the speaker button and held up the phone.

"I'm calling security," Wil said. "You know you're

not supposed to be here. You need to leave now. If you don't—"

There was a loud banging sound. Nick snatched the phone from me. "Judge Brothers! Are you okay? What's going on?"

There was only silence.

Nick pulled a cell phone out of his jacket pocket and quickly dialed a number. "Keep trying to get through to her," he said to me, then he spoke into the phone. "Detective Kingson, Retired, badge number 349201. Possible attack at the courthouse in Judge Brothers' chamber. I was speaking on the phone with her, and I thought I heard shots." He stopped, his eyes meeting mine when someone spoke on his phone. I saw sympathy and a sad knowledge in his gaze. "Thank you." He lowered the phone. "They got a call about shots fired at the courthouse. A unit is on its way there."

I looked at the phone I held, then I shouted, "Wil! Are you there? Talk to me!"

There was silence. Then a whispered voice said, "You need to be careful. Being an heir can be bad for your health."

Chapter 3

I dropped the phone. It bounced off the file papers on the hassock, landing on the floor. Nick scooped it up. "Who is this? Where's Judge Brothers? Wil?"

The only answer was a dial tone. Nick tossed the phone on the chair and dialed again on his mobile phone. "It's Kingson. Get over to the courthouse. Something's going on there." He stopped, turning away from me and going to the front window to stare out. "Damn. Call me when you have details." His slumped shoulders told me all I needed to know.

"She was attacked?"

He nodded, then looked down at me when I joined him. "Security is on the scene and police are on the way. They'll want to talk to you."

"Me? Why?"

"You were the last person to talk to her while she was alive."

I stepped back and sank into the chair. "She's dead?"

"I'm sorry. I shouldn't have phrased it that way. I don't know. My ex-partner is going to call me when he gets any news."

"I need to call Jake," I said. "Someone needs to tell Jake."

"The security at the courthouse will handle that." He looked down at the papers scattered on the hassock.

"What did she tell you?"

I struggled to remember that brief conversation just a few minutes in the past. "She said she wanted me to know this was serious and that I was supposed to take your advice."

"Advice?"

"Something about traveling and meeting the client. I told her I didn't have any plans to travel. That's when I heard her yelling at somebody."

"Did you hear any voices? Anything that might identify who was in her office?"

"No, nothing. I couldn't hear the other person until—" I faltered. "Until that voice at the end." Someone hurt Wil because of me. The knowledge washed over me and I shivered. "What is going on?"

"It's not your fault."

I looked up, startled. "Of course it is. You heard it." My phone, lying on the hassock, rang. I jerked at the loudness. I picked it up warily and checked the caller ID. It was a phone number with the Rampian area code. "Hello?" I said cautiously.

"This is the Rampian Police Department. This number was recently dialed from a crime scene. Who is this?"

Nick pried the phone away from me. "This is Detective Nick Kingson, RPD retired." He moved away and spoke in a low voice, his back to me. Then he handed the phone to me.

"Miss Rampion?"

"Yes, this is she. I was talking to Judge Brothers when she was attacked."

"We need you to make a statement."

"Of course. Can I go to the local police department

in the morning?"

There was a pause. "We'd prefer to talk to you in person."

"You're in Oregon. I'm in Iowa. That's a bit of a trip to make in order to give you my statement." There was something in the peremptory tone of this male police officer that grated on my already tattered nerves.

"I understand, but it's important that we talk to you in person."

The receiver beeped me. I glanced at the display. *Jake cell.* "Excuse me. I have another call I need to take." I didn't wait for the cop's reaction, but switched to the other call. "Jake, this is Punzi. Is Wil okay?"

"How did you know?" Jake sounded rushed, his voice echoing with background noise of a car or maybe traffic.

"I was on the phone with her when she was attacked. Jake, is she okay?"

"I'm on my way to the hospital now. I think it's bad." His voice was shaking. I heard the pent-up grief in it.

"Who's with you? You're not alone, are you?"

"No, security came and picked me up. They'll stick with me until they figure out what's going on. Punzi, this might have something to do with that inheritance."

"I know. While I was talking to her…" I looked up. Nick was shaking his head, his gaze fixed on me while he spoke on his mobile phone. "I heard her being attacked, Jake. Someone came in while we were talking."

"I know it's asking a lot, but can you come out here? I know she'd want to see you, to make sure you're okay. She was worried about the inheritance. She didn't tell me what bothered her, but she said she was concerned. That's why she sent Nick Kingson out there. Hold on." There was a pause. "We're almost at the hospital. Call me later, okay? Or leave a message at the house. Thanks, Punzi. Stay safe."

I lowered the phone, my head spinning. "My God, someone attacked her. Can I find out how she is? Where will they take her?" I stood and walked to the kitchen then turned. "I need to find out where she is."

Nick put his phone back in his pocket. "They're taking her to Portland."

Of course they would. Rampian had a small clinic and hospital, but the specialists that might be needed would be in Portland. "Jake wants me to come out there. I wonder if I should. If this stupid inheritance is involved, I don't want to put anyone else in danger."

"I think you do have to go there. You need to meet with the police. It sounds like Judge Brothers may need you, too."

"I can't just hop a plane. I have a business to run." Even as I said it, I knew I could. Janice could easily manage things while I was gone. "But I owe it to Jake and Wil. I need to be with him to help him." I nodded once. "I'll call the airlines tomorrow and see if I can get a seat on a plane."

"Actually, Judge Brothers reserved a seat for you. It's an open-ended reservation. I was supposed to tell you about it if you decided to get involved with the inheritance investigation."

"Investigation?"

"I'm not sure what else to call it."

"They don't need me for that." I pulled a strand of hair free and extended it toward him. "Just take a sample and we're done."

"It's not that easy. You have to go to a certified lab. Someone there will take a sample. If it matches, then they'll fingerprint you and verify your identity. I doubt they'd trust somebody who just shows up with a lock of hair." He looked down at his phone, tapping at an app. "There's a flight out tomorrow morning from Des Moines. We can take that. It connects in Denver where we change planes."

"I don't think I can leave that fast," I said. "I need to make arrangements."

"How about the afternoon? We'd get in around midnight."

"How about I think about it," I snapped. "I have a lot to process."

"I'm sorry. You're right, of course. Look, I don't mean to be pushy or anything, but I don't like the idea of you being alone." Nick blurted this out in one big rush, like he was afraid I'd interrupt. "With Judge Brothers being attacked and the person on the phone knowing who you are, well, I just don't like it. Do you think I should stay here tonight?"

I considered it. Wil was attacked in Oregon, not Iowa. If she were in the next town, I'd be worried, but she was halfway across the country. True, it was unnerving to think she was attacked while I was talking to her, but no one could have known it was me on the phone.

Then why did they say that about being an heir? A little voice nagged in my head. Maybe she had my file open on her desk. Maybe the person heard her talking to me.

All that flashed through my brain in the time it took

to blink. "I doubt if I'm in danger. I promise I'll lock up behind you and won't open the door for anyone."

He looked like he wanted to argue then he nodded. "It's up to you, of course. But it's just such a coincidence. It bothers me."

"I'm sure it'll be fine."

"Are you going to fly out to Oregon?"

"I don't know. If Jake needs me, then of course I will. He and Wil are the only family I have. I want to see her, but I'm afraid I might put her in danger."

"You see? You're worried, too." He pounced on my words so fast I knew he'd just been waiting for me to say it.

"Yes, I am worried, but I'm worried for her, not me. Look, if it'll make you feel better, I'll watch you in the window while you walk back to the hotel. I'll call you when you get there." I passed him and went into the living room to the front window. "I can see all the way across the square from here."

He turned out the light next to the couch and joined me. "You can, can't you?"

"Yep."

"Okay. But make sure to lock up. And put my phone number on speed dial in case you need it." He waited until I picked up my mobile phone, then he recited his number, verifying it after I entered it.

"Thanks for checking on my intruder." I edged toward the staircase.

We had one of those odd little moments when he went to one side and I did the same, almost colliding. "Maybe it was just a trick of the light because of the snow." He paused at the top of the steps.

"Probably." I led the way down to the store then

through the dimly lit interior to the front door.

"Lock up behind me," he cautioned.

"I will. Thanks." I hesitated. "Thanks for being with me when I heard about Wil. She's like a big sister to me."

"I know." He went outside and tugged his coat collar higher around his face. "I'll see you tomorrow. I'll stop by and we'll firm up our travel plans."

I wasn't sure we would, but I nodded agreement. I closed the door and turned the dead bolt, then slipped the security chain on. I watched him walk to the next tier of houses, then I went back upstairs, crossing my now darkened apartment to stare out the front window.

Nick walked with long strides along the sidewalk, crossing the quiet street to go through the square. How odd to think that he was the same policeman who had helped me so long ago. I had successfully put my past behind me, but today it was suddenly front and center.

When I was relocated, I was given a new identity. I was also given just bits and pieces of information about the people involved with me in my previous existence. Dr. Thell was handed a relatively light prison sentence. Her lawyers successfully argued that her mental health had been impaired by the demands placed on her by the university.

I suppose my testimony helped support that notion because I was asked if she ever discussed the school. I naively said she was unhappy there because of so much emphasis on research and how she was worried about her job. She was sentenced to ten years in a psychiatric facility and died shortly after her incarceration.

I didn't begrudge her the soft punishment. She had treated me coldly but competently. It wasn't until she discovered I'd had sex with Bobby that she became deranged. I think it was some kind of puritanical punishment. Or maybe some kind of twisted jealousy. I was an amazingly beautiful woman-child. I think she envied me my appearance.

If I had any horrible memories, they were caused by Bobby, whose last name I didn't learn until I testified at his trial. He seduced me, toyed with me, and used me, then ran away when Dr. Thell attacked me. I didn't even know he'd been wounded until months later when I had to testify.

Wil pressed for a charge of rape, but I was my own worst witness in that respect. I had willingly participated in sex with him, but I didn't understand the possible consequences of the act. I was of age and that's what the defense attorney kept reiterating. Wil kept repeating that while I was seventeen and technically of the age of consent, I had the cultural and social knowledge of a child.

I gave my deposition to a sympathetic judge and did not have to appear in court. I was still acclimating to the world and Wil kept me sequestered from the legal maneuverings. She didn't count on Bobby's powerful father and his connections. Mr. Reagan hired the best lawyers, mounted a public relations campaign, and effectively painted a picture of me as seductress and his son as victim.

I didn't know any of this. Wil hid it all from me for years. I never knew what became of Bobby or Dr. Thell or the young policeman who helped me. I had to recover from a wound and the complications that arose after a D&C procedure, which left me unable to bear children. I was ill for months and was so physically and psychologically battered that it took several more months for me to recover. By then I didn't really care. My past was behind me, and I was trying to navigate my way in a strange new world.

My mobile phone, sitting on the end table, vibrated and rang, startling me. I fumbled for it and saw Nick's name on the display. "I thought you were going to call me," he said when I answered.

I didn't dare say I was daydreaming while I watched him. He'd probably turn around and come back. "Sorry, I have all the lights off and couldn't find my phone."

There was a suspicious pause then he said, "Keep it near you and call me if you have any worries at all."

"I will."

"Promise me." He laughed. "I told Judge Brothers I'd look out for you. I feel like I owe it to her to hold up my part."

"I promise," I said. "I'm going to sleep now, but I'll keep the phone handy."

"Okay. Thanks for having dinner with me tonight. I enjoyed it."

"I did, too. Thanks for inviting me. I'll talk to you tomorrow."

"Okay. Think about going out to Rampian. I'm sure Judge Brothers' husband would like your company."

"I'll consider it. Good night."

"Good night, Jessa."

I went into the bathroom and got ready for sleep, then went to the bedroom, putting the phone on the nightstand before I undressed. I slipped into bed and leaned back, glimpsing faint light from the third floor of the hotel across the square. I envisioned Nick standing there, phone in hand, while he glared at my house.

It was nice to have someone worry about me, I

decided.

The next day dawned bright and clear, which meant it was also cold. I came downstairs and got the coffee going, then checked the sidewalk. The high school kid we hired to shovel had done his job, and it was safe to navigate.

"So how was the big date last night?" Janice demanded the minute she entered the store from the back door.

"It was odd," I said. "The meal was fine, but Nick insisted on walking me home."

"You walked? I told you to drive," she chided.

"It's just a couple of blocks. Anyway, he walked me home, and I thought I saw someone duck around the side of the building. Or something," I added, not quite sure what it was that had roused my suspicions the night before. "He looked around the shop and didn't see anything wrong. Then Wil called." I stopped, realizing I didn't know her status.

"What about her?"

"I need to call Jake," I mumbled, reaching for my mobile phone. "Wil was attacked last night when she was talking to me on the phone."

"What?" Janice sank down in the guest chair on the other side of my desk.

"I can't believe I didn't think about it. I hope she's okay. I need to call Jake." I found his number in my contact list and pressed the icon to dial it. The phone rang several times, then went to his voice mail. "Jake, this is Jessa. Please call me when you can. I'm worried about you and Wil." I ended the call and dropped the phone on my desk.

"I was talking to her and I heard her. She was in her

office. I think someone attacked her. That's what it sounded like."

"Wow. I read a story in the newspaper the other day. These stupid white supremacist groups have been targeting judges that they think are too liberal. I wonder if that's what happened?" Janice shook her head. "I don't understand that kind of hatred. Are people so stupid they'll fall for all that bullshit you see on those far-right news channels? You know the ones? I've heard about that, how they think there's a secret group of pedophiles running a child sex-trafficking ring and how Trump was going to stop some kind of coup attempt. How stupid can somebody be?"

"Pretty damn stupid. Too many people believe all they hear and see on TV without using the brains God gave them."

"Or didn't give them." Janice got to her feet. "If you need to go out to Oregon, you go right ahead. I'll take care of things here for you."

I sighed, letting my rigid shoulders relax. "Thank you. I think I might have to. The police out there want to talk to me because I was on the phone with her." My mobile phone rang, and I saw Jake's photo on the display screen. I snatched up the phone. "Jake, I was trying to get in touch with you."

"She died a couple of hours ago." Jake's voice was raw with grief. "They took her into emergency surgery but there was too much damage." He drew in a long, ragged breath. "She was shot, Punzi. The bullet missed her heart but punctured her lung. They couldn't—" Whatever he wanted to say ended with a sob.

"Oh, God." I leaned forward, resting my head on my hand. Wil dead. I couldn't imagine it. "Do they know who did it? Why they did it?"

"No to both questions. The police are working on it. There were security cameras in the building. They're hoping to find something there that will help. Punzi, she wanted you to come out here. Will you? I'd like to have you here. I'd like to have family around me."

"Yes," I said immediately. There was no question. I looked up to find Janice watching me. She nodded decisively. "I'll come as soon as I can. I'll talk to Nick about it. He said there was a ticket reserved for me."

"Oh, Wil," Jake said softly. "Of course she planned ahead. What am I going to do without her, Punzi?"

I squeezed my eyes shut against my tears. "I don't know, Jake. We'll have to figure that out, I guess."

"There's a public memorial service on Saturday afternoon. It's being organized by the staffers in Wil's office."

"So soon?" It seemed indecently quick to have a service.

"I think they were worried if we waited, it might get lost in the shuffle around the holidays. We'll have a private service on Sunday just for the family. She'll be cremated. I want to take her ashes to Mt. Hood in the spring. We used to have a spot there where we picnicked." He paused. I knew memories were swamping him just like they were inundating me. "I have a million things to take care of here. Call me when you can and let me know when you'll arrive, okay?"

"I'll call Nick when we hang up," I said. "I'll get the details from him."

"Good. He's good people, Punzi. I've worked with him for years. Make sure you follow his advice."

"What kind of advice? Do you think Wil's death was

related to all this inheritance stuff?"

"I don't know. But I don't want to take any chances. Nick will make sure you get here safely. We can work it all out once you're here."

"Jake, I'm not sure I want my hair to be tested." I decided I needed to get that out in the open quickly. "I don't care about any estate."

He was silent for a long few seconds. "I understand how you feel, but try to think of it from the old man's point of view. He's been haunted by guilt all these years. He made a promise to his dying wife that he would find you and care for you."

"He must not have looked very hard," I snapped. "There was a lot of publicity when I was found."

"Your mother died shortly after they gave you up. He was in and out of treatment for years after that. His family put him in an institution in England, I think. Then he was out of the country, managing his late wife's estate. I think now that he's approaching his own end of life, he wants to make things right. I can understand that. Wil and I talked about it. The older you get, the more you wonder what you did right and what you did wrong in life."

I didn't say it, but I didn't dwell on things like that. Perhaps it was my unconventional upbringing, but to me, the past was dead and gone. I remembered a long-ago psychotherapist who counseled me after I was discovered. He had advocated a forward-facing philosophy and perhaps it rubbed off on me. "I'll think about it. The money just isn't that important to me."

"I know. We'll talk about it when you get here. I need to go now. Leave me a message once you know your flight times. I'm glad you're coming, Punzi."

"I'll call soon. Don't worry, Jake. We'll get through it together."

"Thanks." He hung up.

I dropped my phone to the desk and buried my face in my hands. It was incomprehensible. Wil was dead. Murdered. Good God. Who would do such a thing? Why? Was it some deranged person, angry with one of her verdicts? The minute I considered it, I dismissed it. Wil didn't handle many criminal cases. Of course, given the political climate in the country now, it might have been any lunatic fringe person with a grudge. It seemed like people were willing to believe any crap they read on those ludicrous message boards, the ones that insisted an election was a fraud and a president was the savior of the world. Yes, now that I thought about it, there probably was some unbalanced idiot out there who targeted her because of Wil's interpretation of the law.

"You're flying out to Oregon?"

I looked up. Janice stood in the doorway, regarding me with sad sympathetic eyes. "Yeah. There's some kind of memorial service on Saturday for the public, then a private thing on Sunday for the family. I need to be there."

"Of course you do. I'll handle everything here, so don't worry about that. Will you have time to go over the coupon giveaway with me before you go?"

"Oh, damn," I groaned. I had put an ad in several metro newspapers with a coupon based on a sliding scale. The more you spent, the bigger the discount. It was going into effect tomorrow, on Friday. It would run through the weekend along with the other sales being offered by other stores in town. "Sure, we can work that out. Let me call Nick first. He mentioned something about plane tickets last night."

"I'll call my sister-in-law Shirley and see if she can work this weekend," Janice said. "I'll bet we get busy what with Christmas and the sales going on in town."

"I'm sorry. This is probably going to be one of our busiest weekends."

Janice waved a hand. "Better that than sitting around and being bored. Shirley loves to help out. It'll give us a chance to get caught up. I haven't seen her for a few weeks. She's looking for any excuse to get out of the house now that my brother is retired." She bustled away, pulling her cell phone out of a pocket.

I found Nick's number on my phone and tapped it.

"I was just going to call you," he said. "I talked to Jake. I'm sorry, Jessa. I know how much Wil meant to you."

I struggled to hold back my tears. "I was lucky she was assigned to my case," I whispered. "I owe her so much. And the absolute least thing I can do is fly out there to attend her memorial service. Jake said they're planning something for Saturday."

"He mentioned it to me. I'll call around and see what I can find for flights. We'll probably have to fly out of Des Moines. Cedar Rapids would be too restrictive."

That meant a two-hour drive to get to the airport. Well, it couldn't be helped. "That makes sense. There are lot more flights in and out of Des Moines. I need to spend today getting things ready so I can leave tomorrow."

"Oh. I was hoping we might—"

"No," I said firmly. "Tomorrow."

"Okay. I'll call you when I find us a flight."

"Thanks, Nick. I appreciate it."

"You're not the only person Wil helped. I'm glad to

do it. I'll call you later."

I lowered the phone and pulled over a notepad. I had a lot to do and just a few hours to do it in. I needed to get started.

I spent the morning with Janice in between helping customers. We surveyed our inventory and came up with a pricing plan for the weekend's sale and also what items might be excluded. I spent the afternoon handling bills and other business, then I typed up the details we discussed while Janice helped customers. Then we closed the store for a quick dinner in my apartment to go over the plans with Janice's sister-in-law.

Shirley was a bustling, energetic wisp of a woman with beautifully coiffed white hair and a flamboyant fashion sense. I knew I was leaving the store in very capable hands, and I knew they were looking forward to a busy weekend. They went back to the store for our Thursday evening hours while I tackled the question of what to pack.

I checked the weather in Oregon for the weekend, and like I expected, it was rain with a chance of snow. A pair of dark pants and a dark sweater-set would work for the memorial service with another sweater for Sunday. A couple of pairs of jeans, a casual sweater, and a fleece top were added to the carry-on bag. I rounded up my cosmetics and toiletries and by seven-thirty I was done.

I sat down at my computer and did a bit of google searching. It was surprising how easy it was. I typed in my supposed father's name with Rampian the town name, and I found all kinds of information. I studied the pictures, some from decades earlier. August Miller was a handsome man, with swept-back light brown hair, bright blue eyes, and the sort of chiseled good looks that

I associated with movie stars. If his hair had been just a tad less curly he might have passed for Rob Lowe.

His second wife had her share of pictures, too. Stephanie "Steffi" Bose was a statuesque woman, tall and somewhat broad-shouldered with long chestnut-brown hair that fell in a straight line to her shoulders. She had sculpted cheekbones and a slight tilt to her eyes that gave her an unusual distinctive look. I didn't think she was pretty. But she had presence and the sort of haughty demeanor that I associated with people who felt they were better than the hoi polloi. From what I could glean from the few news stories I found, she was thirty years younger than Miller, which meant she was around my age now, because he was almost ninety.

There were two children, Wanda and Richard. They were in their thirties. From what I could tell, Wanda didn't do anything except appear at social events. There was no mention of occupations or a career. Richard was a state senator and one of the rising stars of the Republican party. I pushed away from the computer and went to the window. I had nothing in common with those people, and I had no desire to meet them. Despite what Jake said, I was not going to let them test me.

I was just finishing my googling when Janice called up the stairs that she was leaving. "I'll take good care of things while you're gone," she said.

"I know you will. You and Shirley have fun."

"Oh, we will! I'll lock up tight."

"Thanks, Janice." I heard the bottom door close and lock, then my cell phone rang. "Hi, Nick," I said.

"I'm sorry I'm so late getting back to you. I had to do some calling around to get us on a flight tomorrow. We're leaving out of Des Moines at nine in the morning."

"Okay. That means we should leave here by six in order to clear security."

"Yeah, that's what I figured. I'll pick you up at five-thirty if that's okay. I have to return the rental car."

"No, that won't work," I said. "You won't be coming back here so I should take my car. I'll need it when I fly back here. I can just follow you."

"I don't think that's a good idea. It's too easy to get separated on the road."

"If we get to the airport around the same time, it should be fine. It's not that big of an airport. I'll just wait for you at the rental car area and we can go up and board together." I walked to the window and stared out at the snowy landscape. Lights flickered in the hotel across the square. Was he pacing in front of one?

"I'd rather we went together. Can't Janice come and pick you up when you fly back?"

"Maybe, but I'd rather not impose on her." His insistence was starting to wear on my already worn nerves. "I don't know why it's a problem."

"Look, you were threatened. I promised Wil that I'd take care of you. Will you please let me do that?" He sounded as peeved as I felt.

I remembered Jake's admonition to trust Nick's advice. "Okay," I said reluctantly.

"Good. Make sure to lock all your doors and check them. If you have any problems tonight, call me."

"Sure."

"Thanks for letting me help, Jessa. I'll see you tomorrow." He hung up before I could reply.

I lowered the phone and went back to my chair, picking up the legal papers I'd dropped there the night before. If I was going back to the past, I guess I needed to be prepared. I settled down to read.

Chapter 4

I was waiting for Nick at the shop's back door the next morning, my carry-on bag at my feet. I saw him pull into the parking lot. I hurried out, locking the door behind me. When I did, I found a small paper bag dangling from the doorknob. The bag had a fat snowman on the front with squirrels cavorting around him. I took the bag and my duffel and started for the sidewalk leading to the lot.

Nick met me halfway, reaching for my carry-on bag. "Thanks for agreeing to let me drive," he said, swinging the small bag like it weighed nothing.

"I guess I still don't understand why it's a concern. I'm not accustomed to worrying about stuff like that." I slowed down when we approached the part of the sidewalk that was in perpetual shadow during the winter. "Be careful here. It melts and refreezes in this spot."

Nick held out his hand and I took it, moving cautiously over the thin slick film of ice. "Whoever does your shoveling does a good job. There's not much to be done for this bit, though." We navigated the tricky patch and safely reached his car, a small SUV.

"I have a high school student handle the mowing and the snowing. That's what he calls it. He's done it for me since junior high. I'll miss having him around when he goes off to college." I settled in the car, the warmth enfolding me.

Nick stowed my duffel in the back then slid into the driver's seat. "What's in the bag?"

I peeked inside. "It's from Janice." I read the slip of paper on top of the tissue-wrapped gifts within. *Don't worry about us while you're gone. I hope you have a safe trip and come back to us a millionaire, so we can buy another store for me to manage. I'm including a good-luck charm to make sure it happens. I know it works because I have one like it, and it helped get me a job with you, and that's been just about the best luck I could have. I hope you find what you need to find. Let me know if I can help.*

The note was signed with a big loopy happy face. I pulled out two enormous muffins in plastic wrap and a keychain with a cat, fat and orange, dangling from it. The cat had its left paw raised, its head back. It appeared to be smiling with its eyes closed. "It's from Janice. She's been after me to get a shop cat. This is her way of reminding me."

"A shop cat? That's a good idea." Nick looked at the little figure. "That's a Japanese good-luck charm. Left paw raised. That means it's good for business."

"Really? There's a difference?"

"Sure. Left paw raised means it's beckoning customers to you. Right paw raised is to bring in money. Left paw for business, right paw for home." He drove out of the parking lot. "Should I just take the Interstate or is there a better route?"

"The Interstate should be fine this time of day." I settled back in the seat, tapping the knob on the dash to adjust its warmth. "How do you know so much about Japanese good-luck figurines?"

"My mother had a collection of them. They're called

maneki-neko. My mom used to love corny things like that. It drove my stepfather crazy. I never understood why they got married because he had all these ideas about what was socially correct, and Mom kept doing stuff that he thought was socially incorrect." He glanced at me. "I think my mom did things just to peeve him and he knew it."

I held up the figurine, letting it sway with the movement of the car. "The thing with a cat in the store is if someone is allergic, it can cause issues."

"Just put a sign in the window and let folks avoid the store if they need to. There's a used bookstore in Portland I love to go to. They have two shop cats. It's nice to sit down in front of a fireplace, skim through some books, and see a cat curled up napping. It's relaxing. Kind of homey."

"That's what Janice says."

He held out his hand and I put the tiny cat on his palm. "I think I've seen this one. Yeah, this one has a warning whistle." He handed it back to me. "If you press the symbol on the front, it lets out a noise to scare away any would-be attackers."

My finger hovered over the symbol but I restrained myself. "Trust Janice to get me something that will bring in customers and keep me safe."

"She has your best interests at heart. You're lucky to have such a good employee."

"I know. I'm glad she likes working there. She's really more than an employee. She can run the place without me." I held up one of the muffins. "I'll hold on to these until we get someplace we can sit and enjoy them. These are her famous orange cranberry muffins. They're messy but good."

"I look forward to it." He made a left turn at the highway, and we were soon driving through the darkness of an Iowa winter morning. "I always forget how black it is in the country at night," he said after a few minutes. "It feels like you're the only person alive in the world."

"I know. Last year when we had the derecho come through we lost power for almost a week. That's something that many people mentioned. They'd go outside at night and see so many stars. A lot of folks who live in town never really see them. But with the lights out for miles around, it made for some good views at night."

"I heard about that. It was quite a storm."

"It's hard to describe. If it were light out now, you'd see the aftereffects for yourself in those woods." I pointed to the dense strand of timber ahead and on the right side of the road. "Probably half of those trees came down. Most farmers with timber stands haven't bothered to clean up the mess. Most of them had all they could do to handle the damage to the crops." I peered into the darkness when we drove by the small forest. "We were lucky it hit in August and we weren't in the middle of a heat wave. It stayed relatively cool for the first week, so we could sleep outside or in the basement, and we didn't miss the air conditioning so much."

"I've never been involved in a natural disaster," Nick said. "Just manmade ones."

I looked at him in the half-light from the dashboard. "What kind is that?"

His hands opened and closed on the steering wheel. "I was a cop. I saw a lot of manmade pain." There was a world of memory in his voice.

What would it be like to be constantly reminded of man's inhumanity to man? I turned my gaze back to the world outside. Wouldn't that affect how you lived and loved and viewed other people? I didn't know what to say.

"I suppose that's why I like it when I see things like shop cats in a bookstore," he continued. "It makes me realize that there is a normal world out there, a world like what people write about in books. Something nice and warm and good." He glanced at me and I saw his self-deprecating smile. "Just call me an old romantic at heart."

"Nothing wrong with that," I murmured. "I had such an odd start in life that I have no idea what's normal and what isn't. I think that gave me an unusual advantage in the world. I was able to form my own ideas and opinions without a lot of outside influence."

"I'm glad you can see it that way. What happened to you was a travesty." His voice was so harsh I flinched. "Reagan preyed on you. Given his history, he shouldn't have been walking around free much less free to do what he did to you."

The memories of that long-ago "relationship" had faded. I didn't feel the anger or guilt that I once had. Anger because I had been manipulated and guilt because I allowed it to happen. It took a long time for me to realize that I had no reason to feel guilty. My counselor slowly and gently led me through my feelings, showing me how the legal officials around me had colored my memories so the guilt crept in. It was just the way society viewed rape and rape victims, especially if the victims were female. There was always a subtle sense of "I should have stopped it." That turned the attacker into the victim and turned the victim into what was viewed as an unwilling partner, not someone whose world was brutally upended.

That's what happened with me. I was initially hospitalized and then kept sequestered so I didn't participate in Bobby Reagan's trial except for the deposition I gave the judge from my hospital bed. But I read the summary Wil prepared for me. She gave it to me when I finished college and was getting ready to set out on my own. I was twenty-four years old. I was both anxious to leave and frightened to leave the home she and Jake gave me during my recovery.

Bobby Reagan had been portrayed as an upstanding young man, a pillar of the community, and a boy with a shining future ahead of him. The fact that he was twenty-four and I was sixteen was glossed over. So were his previous brushes with the law for drunken behavior, bullying, and four other assaults on girls that were dropped by victims after his father paid them substantial amounts of money.

None of that previous behavior was allowed at the trial. Bobby's defense attorney was clever and well-paid. Wil did manage to insert some of the history, which probably was the only reason he got a year in jail for rape and assault. My subsequent pregnancy and miscarriage and near death had also had an effect on the judge who handled the sentencing.

It was years later that I found out the judge had been ousted from his position by a well-managed and well-financed campaign against him during re-election. Reagan's father had orchestrated it, of course. He tried to do the same with Wil, but her bosses in the district attorney's office fought back and word of Bobby's exploits were leaked to the press. His father backed down, but I always wondered if Wil's career didn't suffer in small ways because of her defense of me and her prosecution of Bobby Reagan.

"I'm sorry," Nick said, snapping me out of my memories. "I didn't mean to rake up old wounds."

"No, that's okay," I said quickly. "It was forty years ago. I moved on from all that a long, long time ago."

"I wish I could," Nick said softly. "I wish I'd gotten there sooner."

"I'm lucky you got there when you did." I patted his hand, resting on the steering wheel. "If not for you, I would have died."

"It shouldn't have happened."

"No, but it did. And we're here to tell the tale, so let's just count our blessings." I held up the keychain and the small cat. "Maybe I should get a cat. I'll talk it over with Janice."

"Get an older one," Nick advised. "A kitten might cause a mess in that shop of yours. Too many fun things to play with."

I could easily imagine a cat bouncing around the store, lying on the tablecloths and knocking over some of the bobcat figurines. "Maybe a senior cat," I murmured, tucking the little charm into my purse.

We fell silent, each of us busy with our own thoughts. I stared at the Interstate traffic and tried to imagine what Jake was going through. He and Wil had been married for decades after dating in college. They went through their entire lives together, from the poor days when they lived on spaghetti to now when they were relatively well-off and had a nice home in one of the better parts of town.

I had never had a person in my life the way Wil had with Jake. My few short-lived relationships fell apart before they could become serious, usually because I wasn't comfortable sharing details of my past. That emotional wall on my part became emblematic of my failure to trust my partner. My last lover left me almost six years earlier. I realized when he was gone that I was far happier without him in my life. I just didn't have the desire to compromise and adapt to another person.

"Take the next exit," I said. "There's a better route to the airport than going through town. That road bypasses most of the city so it's a bit faster."

"Thanks." We were soon going south. "How much farther?"

"Maybe twenty minutes or so." He smiled. "What?"

"I noticed that people out here do that. They tell you the distance in time not the miles."

"I never noticed that, but you're right."

"I wouldn't do that in Portland because depending on the time of day, it might vary by an hour or more."

"I don't miss living in the city. I enjoy a slower pace of life."

"What if—what if you do inherit the money? Will that change how you live?"

I considered his question. "I doubt it. I think I've found my niche. I might travel, but it's gotten so odd since the pandemic I'm not sure I'd enjoy it. I'm afraid the days of carefree vacations might be behind me." I pointed ahead. "That's the exit for the airport. Bear left and we can go to the rental car return. It's right next to the terminal."

"If you're a millionaire, you can probably fly first class and rent out a whole hotel if you want it."

"But where's the fun in that? Yeah, flying first class has its appeal, but most of the fun on a vacation is going off the beaten path. It's all a moot point anyway. I'm not going to be tested for some old man who has a guilty conscience."

Nick was silent for a minute or two then he said, "If the old man is dying, where's the harm in helping him die knowing he did right by his late wife?"

"Like I said before. He had years to do it, and now on his deathbed, he decides to do the right thing." I turned to stare at the rows of rental cars lined up and waiting for their drivers. "It must not be that important to him if he can put it off until he dies."

Nick navigated to the correct lane for rental car returns and we went through the process of receipts and surrender of the vehicle. He pulled a suitcase and my duffel from the back hatch of the car and we walked to the ramp leading to the terminal. "You must have been planning on a stay," I said, nodding to his suitcase.

"I always have to check a bag," he replied. "I can't do carry-on if I want to carry a weapon."

I stopped, my eyes so wide it was probably comical. "A gun? You're carrying a gun?"

He nodded. "In the suitcase. It's aviation regulation."

"But why?"

"I suppose they're worried about terrorists and other bad people."

I slapped him on the arm. "You know what I mean. Why are you carrying a gun?"

"I always carry a gun. Where it's legal," he hastened to add. "I've been carrying a gun for almost forty years. It wouldn't feel right to be without one."

"But—but—" I struggled to form a question. "But why?"

"Like I said. I've seen a lot of manmade pain. I always feel better if I'm somewhat prepared for it." He continued walking.

I followed, barely noticing when we entered the main building and joined the few travelers at this hour of the morning. I suppose it made sense because he'd been a cop for so long, but I had never been around anyone who routinely carried a gun. That I knew of, I realized. Iowa allowed open or closed carrying of firearms. I had never seen anyone openly armed, but for all I knew, people were walking around armed to the teeth. It was a sobering thought.

We went up a level. Nick went immediately to the ticketing counter, bypassing the plebian lanes and heading for the VIP desk. I trailed behind him and watched him hand over a form to the woman on duty at the desk. She had him step to the next lane and he did so, putting his suitcase on the weighing machine. He opened the case. I saw a container of some kind sitting on top of his clothing. A steel cable looped through a slot in the container into the frame of his suitcase.

The ticket agent put a bright orange label on the container and Nick closed the bag. Then he paid a fee and took the baggage claim check from the woman in addition to some other kind of form. She directed us to a special TSA inspection area where Nick once again opened the bag. This time he also opened the container. He stood back and we watched the agent inspect the gun and what I assume was ammunition in the case. When they were done, they put another card into the case. Nick closed it and locked it, then he also closed and locked the suitcase, and the agent whisked it away. The whole process took about twenty minutes.

"You can go through here for security screening, sir," the TSA agent said. We handed over our identifying papers, then my duffel and Janice's food sack trundled through the X-ray machine. In a few minutes, we were in the main terminal.

"Do you do that often?" I asked, juggling my purse and my duffel.

Nick took the duffel from me and slung it on his shoulder. "Any time I fly. It's a pretty simple process. Somebody may inspect it in Denver when we change planes for Portland. If they do, they'll put another card into the suitcase so I know it."

"And then you just grab the bag off the conveyor belt like the rest of us?"

"No, it's usually kept in the security office until I can claim it and show them my ID. Do you want some coffee to go with our muffins?" Nick paused outside a coffee shop.

"Sure." We got into line and soon were strolling through the terminal, looking for a likely spot to sit down. The place was surprisingly busy, but it was a Friday, and I suppose business travelers were returning home and other travelers were leaving. We ended up finding a small table outside our gate and settled down to eat. The muffins were excellent and just sticky enough to be messy.

"You don't need to worry about the fact I have a gun," he said. "For a lot of people, it's just a regular part of life."

I had always associated guns with either law enforcement or crazy, far-right assholes like the ones who attacked the Capitol building during Trump's disastrous presidency. Nick was retired from the police, so why did he still feel the need to carry a weapon? I realized that I didn't know much about him. For all I knew, he was one of those loony conspiracy theorists. "I don't understand the need to carry a gun," I said. "It's completely different than anything I was raised to believe in."

"You mean by Dr. Thell?"

"No, by Wil and Jake," I snapped. "I credit them with really raising me."

"I'm sorry. I didn't mean to hit a nerve. It's just that you're judging me based on a simple thing like me carrying a gun."

"I guess I'm one of those people who view guns as a problem, not a solution."

"Perhaps you feel that way because you've never been in a situation where a gun solved a problem," he said quietly. "That might change your opinion."

"I can't even imagine a situation like that, so maybe you're right." I peered over his shoulder then stood. "I think I'll use the restroom before we board."

Nick bundled up the debris of our meal and fell into step with me. "I'll just wait for you here," he said, leaning against the wall outside the ladies' room.

I knew it was useless to argue with him, so I went inside. Our conversation had unsettled me. Perhaps it was because he seemed so serious about this whole inheritance business. Or maybe it was because I was traveling with a stranger and I wasn't sure I liked him. I felt like a small part of his personality had been revealed, and I didn't like what I saw. But I suppose he could say the same thing, I realized. I stared at myself in the mirror. I was a stranger to him. He felt obligated to help me because of Wil. He was probably looking forward to this trip being over and getting on with his normal life, whatever that was.

I left the restroom and Nick fell into step with me without speaking. We went to the boarding area and didn't have long to wait until our flight was called. "A chance to try first class," Nick said with a smile. "Judge Brothers insisted on it."

I imagined Wil's laughing expression when she made the arrangements. I knew what she'd say. "You only go around once, Punzi. Enjoy the ride." I nodded mutely, getting in line with Nick while I blinked back tears.

I had never flown first class and even though it was a small plane, the difference was noticeable, both in the comfort of the seats and the amenities offered. I settled back with a complimentary mimosa and an assortment of cookies, determined to enjoy the experience.

We were soon airborne. I leaned back my seat, looking down at the Monopoly-sized real estate below. Whenever I flew, I stared out the window wondering who was out there, what did they did for a living, and what their day would be like. The small cars moving on the county roads and highways all seemed to be so intent and purposeful as if they were aimed at a target and on their way to some adventure. In reality, the occupants were probably going to school or work, but it was fun to imagine other outcomes for them.

What would my day be like, this Friday unlike all others? What would it have for me? Grief, certainly. And what else? A new family complete with father and stepmother? I couldn't imagine it. I shied away from that idea and focused on Wil. She was the reason for this trip, not some amorphous father figure who felt guilt pangs about my life.

Wil had been my guide, my mentor, and my role model. I had nothing when I came out of isolation, no guidelines or purpose for the new world ahead of me. Wil and Jake stepped in and filled those gaps for me. I could never fully repay her, but I could honor her memory. I also owed it to Jake, who allowed me into their inner circle and accepted me.

I closed my eyes and tried to relax. I knew it might be my last chance to do so for a long time. But when I did, I saw Wil's face. She wasn't pretty in a conventional sense with her short-cropped dark hair and triangular face. But the intelligence and humor in her dark eyes and her ready smile always transformed her appearance, making her somehow light up.

A tear rolled down my cheek. Nick's hand covered mine where it gripped the armrest. I didn't open my eyes or acknowledge his comfort, but when I smiled, the weight of his hand increased slightly.

Thank you, I said to Wil's memory. Thank you for sending him back into my life. It didn't matter that I had reservations about him. I needed someone with me to face what was coming. Even though he and I had different backgrounds, I knew he would respect my grief. I knew he would respect Jake's. It was all I could ask of anyone.

The flight to Denver was short, just an hour. We had an hour and a half before boarding for our next flight. "Do you mind if we walk around?" I asked. "I always like to move whenever I can when I fly. It sort of makes up for the time I have to sit still."

Nick looked so relieved I laughed. "I'm glad you want to," he admitted. "I'm usually wedged into a plane seat and feel like I have to unwind myself after a flight. Even the first-class seats aren't made for somebody my size."

We wandered around the terminal, pausing at some of the shops to look at souvenirs and magazines. "We should probably get something to eat," Nick suggested. "Our next flight is almost three hours long, then I'll have to clear security with my bag. Add in the drive to Rampian and that means it'll be three o'clock, but almost five o'clock central time."

I glanced at my watch, which showed eleven o'clock. "Time difference. That's right." I reset it for Pacific time. "We can buy something and take it with us. I'm not very hungry now."

The sandwiches we bought came in handy when our flight was delayed an hour because of mechanical problems. By the time we were circling Portland, it was after two o'clock Pacific time. Nick was right about the delay to get his suitcase. That added another forty-five minutes in the terminal while he waited for security, then opened the suitcase and the interior container to verify the contents. It was almost four o'clock before we started for the doors leading to ground transportation.

We passed several people holding signs with names of people who had probably just landed. I didn't pay attention to any of them until one of the men holding a sign stepped in front of me. "Sherry Miller?" he asked, brandishing his placard.

Nick stepped forward, moving so his body mostly hid me. "We didn't arrange for any transportation."

"Mr. Miller sent a limousine for his daughter." The man, tall like Nick, didn't appear intimidated. He seemed more like a bouncer than a chauffeur.

"My name is not Sherry Miller," I said, talking around Nick's arm. "And I'm not taking a ride anywhere with someone I don't know." I pushed past both men and headed for the exit. Nick caught up to me in a few steps. "How the hell did anyone know I was coming?" I fumed. I shot him a suspicious look. "Who told them?"

"It wasn't me," he said. "August Miller is rich with a capital R. He probably has somebody meeting every flight from the Midwest. They would know you'd fly out here for Judge Brothers's funeral."

"I suppose that's possible. I wouldn't know. I'm not that rich." We emerged from the terminal, pausing at the roadway before crossing the multiple lanes of traffic encircling the airport. "Where's your car?"

"Long-term parking. It's not too far." Nick tugged my duffel away from me and hooked it to his suitcase to roll alongside him. "I'm afraid we'll hit rush hour traffic once we leave here. There's no simple way to get to Rampian without going through town."

"So what you're saying is this is one of those times when you calculate a trip in miles, not time?"

"Yeah, I'm afraid so. It's only forty miles, but—" Nick shrugged.

I was starting to feel the effects of a day of travel. I felt gritty and wrinkled. I wanted a chance to change clothes, wash my face, and stretch out and relax. Then I realized I didn't know *where* I might relax. "I didn't even think about getting a hotel room. I suppose there's a Holiday Inn or something on the way to town."

"Jake made reservations," Nick said without breaking stride. "We're staying at the Rampian Arms."

"*We* are?" I hesitated, and he was several steps ahead before he saw I wasn't nearby.

He turned to look at me. "I told you. Judge Brothers asked me to look out for you. I'll be doing that until we know for sure it's safe."

"When will that be?"

"I don't know. For now, let's just get to the hotel and try to relax. It's been a long day for both of us."

I nodded reluctantly and followed him into the parking lot. When we got to his car, a dark sedan, he put my bag into the trunk, then his, opening it and taking out the gun. I watched him load it and tuck it into the empty holster snugged under his arm. He glanced at me while doing it as though daring me to say anything. I decided not to argue, but just sank down into the seat, wondering how my life had taken such an unexpected turn in a matter of hours.

I remembered my conversation with Janice last night before I went up to my apartment. "You need to play this out," she had said. "It's not about the money. It's about your life. Who you are."

She was right. Who am I? Where did I come from? I needed answers and some measure of closure about my past. The only way to find answers was to face my past. Maybe the answers were here. I wondered if I would like what I found.

Chapter 5

We drove through damp fog, the overcast skies so heavy it felt like the sky was pressing down on us. The moist chill crept into Nick's car, a roomy sedan. I shivered, and he noticed, nudging the heat a notch higher.

"It's odd how I seldom get cold when it snows, but whenever it's cold and rainy, I feel it more. I think it's because it rains so much here," I said. "The snow seemed so clean and pretty the few times it snowed, but the rain always just felt dreary. I used to stare out the window and wonder if there was anywhere in the world where it was sunny. Then I saw a picture of Spain, and I decided that's where the sun lived."

"Have you traveled overseas?"

"No. There were so many other places to see in the U.S. Somehow I never got around to foreign countries."

"It's not too late," he said with a smile.

"I know, but the older I get, the less anxious I am to travel. I guess I've come full circle. For the first years of my life, I never went anywhere. And I'll probably end up the same way."

"That's not so terrible."

"No, if it's your choice it isn't." The heavy traffic around us was moving slowly, the four lanes of the highway clogged with cars. "You were right about rush hour. I thought a lot of people were still working from home." I felt the telltale vibration of my phone in my purse. I pulled it out and looked at it. *Unknown number.* I tucked it away again.

"A lot of businesses did shift over to telecommuting, but many of them have gone back to having people on-site at least part of the time. Plus the university is about two miles that way." Nick nodded to the left. "And the teaching hospitals are on the right, just past that exit. It's always busy around here no matter what time of the day it is."

"I've gotten out of the habit of traffic. I don't think I could live in a big city anymore." I huddled into my jacket as though that would block out the sight of all the cars. "Where do you live? Do you live in Portland or Rampian?"

"I have an apartment in Rampian and an acreage about thirty miles north with a house that's perpetually under renovation." He smiled wryly. "An old man I know owned it and used it as a hunting cabin, so it was pretty rough when I got it. I've been fixing it up and bringing it into the twenty-first century. I have indoor plumbing now and electricity. My Wi-Fi depends on a satellite signal. It's pretty iffy, though, and sometimes the hot water goes on the fritz. I go up there on the weekends and tinker around."

"I was lucky when I found the shop. The former owner had already updated everything, so all I had to do was paint a few rooms and move in."

"It's a lot of work to take care of a store like that. Do your artists work on consignment?"

I was pleased he used the term 'artists'. So many people viewed crafts people as hobbyists no matter how talented they were. "It's a split between the artist, me, and a donation to the Chamber of Commerce to fund publicity and marketing for all the stores. It's worked out well for everybody."

"Lots of bookkeeping, though, right?"

"Yes, but that's where Janice is worth her weight in gold. She's a whiz at managing all that."

"You're lucky to have her. A good worker who's also a good friend is hard to find."

"I know." I tapped my purse. "Plus I have the super good luck charm. That's sure to come in handy." I peered at the skyscrapers ahead of us. "That must be downtown."

"Yep. Once we navigate through that tangle we can head west." He glanced quickly at me then returned his attention to the traffic surrounding us. "Do you remember much about Portland? Did you spend much time in town?"

"No, I stayed with Jake and Wil at their place once I was released from the hospital. I only lived in Rampian for four years."

He glanced at me. "You were living there when I found you."

"I guess I don't count that. I never saw anything more than the back yard, so it didn't feel like I was part of the town."

"The house was isolated," he said. "At least, back then it was. It's been torn down. A couple of years ago."

"Really?"

He nodded. "That whole part of town was changed. There's a school there now and a lot of houses. It's become a real neighborhood."

I remembered the shabby old house with the dilapidated garden in back. The view out my window had the garden, an alleyway, and a commercial building beyond it with trucks that came and went. The few times I was allowed into the front of the house, all I saw was an empty lot across the street and low buildings in the distance. I found out later that was the community college where Bobby went to school. "It wasn't much when I lived there. I didn't know what a real home was like until I went to live with Wil and Jake."

"You stayed with them for four years?"

"I tested out of high school easily, and Wil arranged for me to take college classes online for a year. When I did finally attend class on campus, she went with me at first to help me navigate my way around. I got my B.A. in business administration, and then I got a job offer from a company in Seattle. It was close enough to home but far enough to let me test how to be on my own. Then I got a job in the Midwest and moved out there. She stayed in touch with me the whole time. It was like having a guardian angel watch over me."

"She and Jake are special people. Were special," Nick said softly. "I remember she took me aside before the trial started. She told me I didn't have to testify if I didn't want to. I didn't know that I even had a choice. I was so new to law enforcement and the whole penalty aspect of it. That was the first time I had to testify as a police officer."

"Why would she do that? Tell you that? I mean, why was there a question? Were you worried about telling what happened?"

He froze, hands stiffening on the steering wheel. "It was a high-profile case because of the Reagan family. It might have affected my career. I know some of the officers on the force warned me about that. They said it might come back to haunt me. She bucked the system when she defended you," he said. "Reagan was a powerful man in town. We were lucky that her bosses supported her."

"I didn't realize how it might have affected you. She did tell me that your testimony helped the case and helped me find justice."

"Is that what you got?" Nick stared at the traffic, his face taut and angry. "He got off with a minor offense. A year in prison and then released without even having to register as a sex offender."

"But wasn't he injured? I read in the trial transcripts that he was."

Nick jerked as though I'd pulled him out of some deep thought. "Yes, he was. Your guardian wounded him."

"Guardian. I suppose that's as good a word as any."

"The Reagans moved out of town after the trial. I think they were embarrassed about having a convict for a son. It didn't look good with the country-club set they ran around with."

"I remember Wil telling me that. I was so disoriented at first that I don't know if I even understood what she meant. The concept of someone just packing up and moving somewhere else was so alien to me." *Alien* didn't begin to encompass how confused and stunned I was by the world I discovered outside my tower.

"The last I knew, the remaining family was living in Lake Oswego."

I racked my brain, trying to remember the basic layout of the area.

Nick saw my confusion. "It's the high rent district. Most homes there start at a million, especially if they have lake access. It's south of town."

"Remaining family?"

"The father died. I'm not sure who is left."

We had taken an exit onto a divided highway, two lanes in each direction. It looked somewhat familiar. "I think Wil and I used to drive into campus this way. So much has changed since I lived here, though. I think back then it was just a regular highway, not divided."

"You're right. They had to expand it because so many people live out in the western suburbs now. We still have a downtown, though. It hasn't gotten completely swallowed up." We drove in silence for another ten minutes. Multi-story office buildings and businesses gave way to strip malls and apartments, with an occasional school in the distance. When Nick turned onto Rampian Road, I barely recognized it. Houses stretched on both sides. I could tell they weren't recent, either. Full-grown trees lined the road. "What's all this?"

"The city is expanding out our way. The population's doubled in the past ten years." He drove past the houses. I recognized the elementary school on the left side and the spot where there used to be a dairy where Wil, Jake, and I got ice cream. Their house was another half mile down that road, which used to be gravel in the past. Now it was a tree-lined boulevard with large homes on each side.

We passed a small strip mall with a pizza place, a coffee shop, a burger joint, and a gas station. A few minutes later we were in the town proper, driving through the business district. "Not much has changed," I said, looking at the four blocks of storefronts. "New stores, of course, but the layout's still the same. But there are so many apartment buildings and houses. It was never this densely populated when I was here."

"When they widened the highway, that made this part of town a lot more accessible. We've kind of been swallowed up by Portland." He turned off Main Street onto a street that went up a steep hill. At the top was a small three-story hotel with a bright red awning in front. "This is the newest hotel in town. Jake said he made reservations here." Nick drove behind the building and we parked among the other vehicles already there.

Nick pulled our bags from the car, and we went up the wide stone steps. The lobby was a calm, subdued space with dark flowered carpet, a dark wood counter, and a small fountain bubbling in an atrium straight ahead.

A young man dressed in a starched white shirt, tie, and dark trousers smiled when we approached. "Checking in?"

"I believe Jake Brothers made a reservation for us," Nick said. "Jessa Rampion and Nick Kingson?"

"Yes, we have that reservation. A suite on the third floor. Could you please provide us with some identification?" The young man turned his attention to me. "You have the same name as the town. What a coincidence."

"Similar, but different. My name is spelled with an 'o' not an 'a'."

The man peered at his computer screen. "You're right. Interesting."

"Yes, isn't it," I murmured. "You said it's a suite?"

He smiled politely. "Two rooms with a common living space. Mr. Brothers insisted on it. Are you here for the funeral?"

I fumbled for my driver's license. "Yes, I am."

"Such a terrible thing. Judge Brothers was well liked and well respected." The man took our licenses and passed them under a scanner before handing them back to us. "It shocked the entire town. It happened just a few blocks from here. We expect crime like that in Portland, but here? In Rampian?" He shook his head dolefully while pressing keys. "Such a tragedy."

I glanced at Nick, but he had turned to survey the lobby and the few people walking through it. I glimpsed an interior balcony in the atrium and green plants with chairs spaced at intervals forming little conversation groupings.

"Mr. Brothers left this for you." The desk clerk slid a folded note across the counter with two key cards in paper envelopes. "Your suite is on the third floor. We have five suites on that floor. Yours is the one nearest the elevator as he requested. The elevator is around the corner on the right. If there is anything we can do to make your stay more comfortable, please just let us know."

"Thank you." I took the key cards and handed one to Nick. "I'd rather not be in a suite," I muttered, heading toward the atrium. "A room would be fine."

"Jake has enough to worry about now. I'm sure he just wants to be sure you're okay." Nick led the way through a short hallway to the elevator.

I opened the note. *Thank you for coming, Jessa. I'll call in the morning. I'd like you to come over early so we can talk. Jake.*

I tucked the note in my coat pocket.

"Everything okay?" Nick asked.

"I think so. He'll call in the morning and let us know what time to come over. I don't even know the details about the funeral." I started into the open elevator but

Nick held me back until the door had fully opened.

He peered inside then stepped in, gesturing me to follow. "There's a public visitation tomorrow. I believe there's a private service on Sunday, then Jake said he wants to scatter her ashes in the spring." Nick pressed the button for the third floor. "Jake said he hoped you could stay until at least Monday so he could spend some time with you."

"I suppose I can. It's an open-ended ticket, right?"

Nick nodded.

"What did you mean about making sure I'm okay? Are you worried someone might try to hurt me because of that inheritance?"

"Not really. I think Jake's on edge because of what happened to the judge. You're a single woman traveling alone. I think he just wants to make sure nothing happens to you, too."

I didn't point out that I'd been traveling alone most of my adult life and so far I was fine. If assigning Nick to me made Jake feel better, then I'd accommodate him. Lord knows he had enough other things to worry about. I glanced around the small elevator. It had expensive-looking wood paneling and soft lighting with faint music coming from a speaker overhead. The advertisement on the wall was for the restaurant downstairs, *The Spun Gold Spot.* Odd name, I thought, but it appeared to be somewhat upscale.

The elevator door opened. We stepped into a foyer with two doors on each side and one ahead of us. Nick went to that door and pressed the key card against the lock. He went inside holding up a hand to stop me when I would have followed. "Let me check first," he said then vanished within.

"Check for what?" I took a step into another foyer, this one quite small with a table to my right and closet on the left. Going forward, I entered what looked like a living room with a sofa and two chairs facing a wall of windows. On the left wall was a tiny kitchenette with counter, miniature fridge, and cabinets. On the right was an entertainment area with two chairs in front of a wall-mounted TV.

Nick came out of a doorway next to the kitchenette. "I asked you to wait."

"Oops." I stepped out his way when he crossed the room, going to a door near the television. I went to the room he just vacated, finding a spacious bedroom with a sliding door onto a small balcony overlooking the town below us. An attached bath completed the accommodations.

"Which one do you want?" Nick asked. "This one is probably more girly."

"Girly?" I looked at the dark rose-colored bedspread with a white headboard. "Sure, I'll take the girly one."

He tossed my duffel on the bed. "I'm hungry. How about some dinner in an hour or so?"

"That sounds good. I need to wash my face and lie down for a few minutes."

"I'll get us a reservation." He turned to go.

"Thanks, Nick. For the escort."

"My pleasure." He closed the door softly behind him.

I shook out my packed clothing and hung it up, then washed my face and flopped down on the bed. There was faint light from the bathroom, but otherwise the room was dark and quiet. Images, pieces of conversation, and memories began a march through my brain. I didn't try to corral any of it. Soon my tense shoulders relaxed and I fell into a light doze.

I heard a murmuring, a voice almost too soft to be understood. It was Nick, probably talking on his phone. The voice became clearer, then faded, then was clearer again. He must be pacing, I realized, probably going back and forth in the living area. Poor man. Under so much stress. I wonder why?

"…tell her about it all. It's a mistake not to…"

Tell me what? Was there something I was supposed to know about?

"…don't know where. I'm not welcome there so I can't find…"

Who was he talking to? Nick sounded angry or upset, as if he had to defend himself from whoever was speaking. I yawned and blinked sleepily.

"…can't ask her to do that. It wouldn't be…"

I sat up and swung my legs over the side of the bed. The bedside clock said almost six-thirty. Good heavens, I did sleep a bit.

"I know and I will. I'm sorry, it's just that she's…"

Now he sounded contrite. I considered opening the door and poking my head out but decided it really wasn't my place to intrude. Instead I went to the closet and changed my cardigan and blouse for a collared red sweater. Then I went to the bathroom and pulled my hair out of my customary bun and brushed it. I held it back from my face with a red headband and let it fall in a straight line past my shoulders.

As I was adding on a dab of makeup, my phone vibrated again. *Unknown number.* It looked like the same one as before. I considered answering, but the call ended before I could. I shrugged, finished my ministrations, then left, feeling much better for my brief nap.

When I came out of the bedroom, Nick was standing near the window, hands in his pockets. He'd changed from the blue jeans and jacket he wore on the plane into a tweed suit coat over a dark shirt and black jeans.

"Is everything okay?" I asked, joining him to look at the town below.

"Sure." He turned to smile at me then stopped. "Your hair. It's the same."

"What?"

"It's the same color. I guess I didn't realize that. You've always had it pulled back." He reached out his hand then stopped. "May I?" I nodded. He picked up a strand and held it, letting it run through his fingers. "It's the same. Your hair was so soft and such a beautiful color. She cut some of it off, but you still had one long section that was all coiled up, next to you on the floor."

Lying on the floor next to all the blood. There were times when I still had nightmares about that, about Thell wrapping her hand in my hair and stabbing at it with the scissors. I stepped away from him. "I've never let it get so long since then." I tried a brief smile. "I guess I'm superstitious."

He straightened, his eyes wide. "I'm sorry. I keep bringing up memories that are probably better left behind."

I looked past him to the town. "I'm back where it all started. There are bound to be memories." I picked up one of the key cards laying on the coffee table. "Shall we go see what the Spun Gold restaurant has to offer?"

"I know why it's called Spun Gold." Nick walked with me to the door. "I brought my mother here for an outing. They use spun sugar to make little sculptures for their desserts."

"Well, I'll make sure to save room then." He opened the door for me and looked out into the foyer, then gestured me ahead of him. "Is your mother still in town?"

He closed the door and went to the elevator to tap the button. "She's in an assisted living facility south of here. She's almost ninety, but she's doing very well." The affection in his voice was obvious.

"It must be nice for her to have you so near."

The car came, and Nick peeked inside, then followed me in. "Mom had a tough time of it for a while. My stepfather wasn't the easiest man to get along with. I didn't appreciate all she went through at the time. It wasn't until I was an adult that I understood how hard her life had been, not only with him but before that."

"Are they still in town? Your stepfather and the stepbrother?"

"My stepfather died. I don't stay in touch with my stepbrother."

I once again sensed that wall where his family was concerned. I stepped out of the elevator at the lobby. We followed the sounds of voices to our right where there were tables set among the tall planters scattered around the atrium. A few people were sitting there sipping drinks. The restaurant was set back behind a row of bushy ficus plants, its dark interior private and secluded.

Nick gave our name to the hostess at the door to the restaurant. We were soon seated at a table for two near a window overlooking the terrace where diners probably ate in the summer months. The restaurant was large but not crowded, the tables generously spaced apart and the atmosphere quiet and subdued. My jangled nerves began to relax.

A waiter appeared immediately. We ordered cocktails then turned our attention to the menu. It was a very sparse assortment, all ingredients sourced from local vendors. Our drinks arrived promptly and after some discussion with the waiter we made our selections.

Nick raised his bourbon. "Here's to Wil Brothers," he said softly.

I held up my glass. "To Wil." I took a sip and smiled. "I love a good martini and this is excellent." I set down the drink and broached a subject that had been in the back of my mind for the last two days. "I've been thinking about Wil. Why was she killed? Was it because of me?"

"Don't blame yourself," Nick said. "Judges are always targets of wacko people."

"It's a big coincidence," I pointed out. "What if she had some evidence that proves who I am one way or the other?"

He nodded. I realized he had already thought through a hundred possible motives. He was an ex-cop, and that's probably how he'd been trained. "That's possible, but it's doubtful. Why kill her? Why not hold her hostage until she gives up the evidence?"

"Oh. Yeah. That makes sense, I guess."

"It might be that she personally knew too much," he said. "That whatever she knew might influence the outcome of your case."

"I thought you said I wasn't the cause."

"If you were the cause," he amended. "It's also possible it was someone involved in one of her current court cases and they had a grudge against her."

"I suppose." I wondered if we would ever know. I struggled to recall that phone call and what exactly she'd said. It was so shocking that it wasn't until later I realized there might have been a clue. But I couldn't remember exactly. I sipped my drink, my attention caught by a woman peering through the room, her gaze sweeping over the diners. She was tall, dressed in a sleek winter coat and high heels with dark nylons. When she saw us, she changed direction. "Who's that?"

Nick turned. "Your stepmother. What's she doing here?"

"Stepmother?"

The woman reached us, standing near me on my left. "We were expecting you. Why didn't you take the limousine we provided?"

I regarded her with what I hoped was disdainful incuriosity. "Who are you?"

She stiffened. "I'm Stephanie Bose. August Miller is my husband."

I noticed covert glances shot our way. She was a striking figure and was making no effort to lower her voice or even pretend at privacy. She did look something like the picture I'd found, but this woman was older, more brittle.

"That's irrelevant to me," I said. "I'm not here to see you or your husband. I'm here to support a friend of mine who's suffered a terrible loss."

"Irrelevant?" She tossed her head, long blonde hair tumbling over her expensive jacket. "That's a laugh. I'm sure you're here for one reason and one only. The money. So let's cut to the chase." She leaned closer. A faint odor of apples and some sort of spice wafted around me. "I'll give you one hundred thousand dollars to leave right now."

I weighed several possible answers. *Not enough money if we're talking millions. I told you, I'm here for*

Jake, not for the money. You arrogant bitch, who do you think you are?'

In the end, I said, "I may not be the person you think I am."

Her expertly lined lips thinned. "You look like her."

"Her?"

"The first wife. All it requires is a test to prove it."

I leaned away from her. She looked so manic I wouldn't have been surprised to see a pair of scissors in her hands. I shivered, past memory intersecting the present moment. "I don't want your money. I won't give you my hair."

Nick reached across the table to touch my hand. "Don't say that. You might regret it."

"You don't know me very well," I said softly. "I sincerely doubt I'll regret it."

He snatched back his hand. "I'm sorry."

"Don't be. This is my fight, not yours."

"It's my fight, too." He looked up at Bose. "She said no. So please leave us alone."

"Who are you?"

"A family friend."

Bose laughed. "She has no family. Don't tell me. You're after the money, too."

I stood, tossing down my napkin. "A dear friend of mine is dead. I don't need this kind of bullshit drama." I tried to move past her, but she shifted position and blocked me.

"I'm not done talking to you."

Nick stood. "Yes, you are." He put out his hand.

I pushed forward, looping my arm through his. The flustered waitress appeared, her gaze darting from us to Bose.

"Please send our meal to room service," Nick said. "I'll leave our room number with the hostess."

The girl nodded. "Sure, fine." She turned to Bose. "Will you be dining?"

"Are you insane? In this place?" Bose swept past me, deliberating bumping me, so I ended up pressed against Nick. "I want this settled once and for all," she said, pausing to confront me in the middle of the dining room. "I'll get your hair one way or another."

I started to reply but Nick moved forward, taking me with him. "Let's go, Jessa."

Bose blinked. "I thought your name was Sherry. Augie said that was your name."

"I had no name," I said. "I had nothing from him or my birth mother."

"It was supposed to be temporary. That's what he told the woman, that professor. He told her he would come back for you."

"And I guess he forgot about that, just like he forgot about me." I walked away, my arm firmly held against Nick's body.

"He did. He went back and the professor said she put you up for adoption." Bose trailed behind us, talking loudly.

"What?"

"He went back after she died. After your mother died. He was in bad shape and had to go through treatment. I blame her for what happened to him." Bose darted around us, almost upending a waiter weaving his way through the room. "She got addicted and sucked him down with her. But once she died, he was able to get free and turn his life around."

"He told you that?" I don't know why, but it felt like

a betrayal of the dead woman I never knew.

"No, not in so many words. But I put it together based on the few things he said and his family said. And what some of his business partners have said. He's never said a bad word against her, but I know the memory is painful for him."

We reached the entrance to the restaurant. I finally turned to confront her. "My memories are painful, too," I said. "I was raised by an emotionless madwoman, and I almost died. I came here for one reason and only one reason. To be with a friend and mourn with him because we lost someone we loved. I don't care about you, your husband, or the fucking money. So leave me alone." I turned.

She grabbed hold of my shoulder. Nick took her wrist and wrested her away from me. "It's time for you to leave. Jessa doesn't want to talk to you."

The hostess watched this all with eyes so wide I thought they'd pop. "Should I call security?" she asked tremulously.

"I'm leaving." Bose struggled against Nick's grip. When he released her, she staggered back into the wall. "We need an answer one way or another. If I have to, we'll go to court."

"Why? This makes no sense. I don't want to have anything to do with you. Just leave me alone, and everything will be fine."

"My husband won't rest until he knows one way or another if his daughter is alive."

"Then I guess he'll have to learn to live with not knowing." I spun on my heel and strode out of the restaurant.

Chapter 6

Nick caught up to me a few steps into the area in front of the restaurant. "Come on." He steered me into the bar located next to the restaurant.

I glanced behind me. Stephanie Bose was striding through the lobby, her face red and her entire body radiating rage. The people in her path took one look and went in the opposite direction. She looked like she might explode and didn't care if the shrapnel decimated people around her.

"Let's finish our drinks." Nick tugged me into the dark bar to a table in the corner. He went to the counter and spoke to the bartender then came back with a martini for me and a bourbon for him. "I told them to have room service delivered in a half hour."

"I don't understand." I took a healthy swallow of my drink but barely tasted it. "I told her I want nothing to do with them. Why are they persisting?"

Nick sloshed the bourbon in his glass before taking a sip. "Jake has some theories about that, but I'd rather he talk to you about it."

"What?"

Nick nodded. "Wil had details about what she thinks the family is after. She discussed it with Jake when Miller's representatives contacted her. Jake wants to discuss it with you. That's one reason for the open-ended ticket. She was hoping you'd come out here so she could talk to you. No one expected that she'd be attacked and die. If anyone had even suspected that she might be in danger, we would have had guards with her."

"Wait a minute. You're saying I am the cause of her death." My hand shook so much I had to set my glass down.

"I'm saying we don't know. It's possible. There's a lot at stake."

"There's money at stake," I said. "That doesn't measure up to a person's life."

"To some people it does. There are people who will kill you for the money in your wallet. They have absolutely no sense of the worth of a person's life." His odd eyes burned with intensity. Through a trick of the lighting I could see their disparate colors clearly. "I don't know if your inheritance was directly related to her death, but it's certainly a possibility."

I looked away, staring without seeing at the bottles of liquor lining the mirror behind the bartender. "It's just money," I repeated. "I don't understand any of this. I don't understand violence."

"There's nothing to understand. Sometimes people are assholes." Nick's voice was low and harsh. I knew he was speaking from horrible experience.

As abnormal as my memories were, I suppose his were far worse. I felt guilty for bringing up such a topic. "I had such an odd childhood, so I think that's given me a whole different perspective on the world."

"I suppose it did. I wondered..." He looked at me then away.

"What?" I prompted.

"I never understood why you—how Bobby Reagan—why you didn't..." He looked embarrassed and unsure of himself, an oddly charming combination.

I was grateful for a change of subject, anything to divert my thought from the idea I might have caused Wil's death. "I knew about sex. Dr. Thell made sure I understood the mechanics. But I had no idea about the emotions surrounding it. I was right in the middle of puberty. Ironically enough, my actions were enough to prove to her that nature triumphs over nurture. She never discussed the ramifications of sex with me. Oh, I knew about pregnancy, but it seemed a relatively minor consequence from what I read."

Nick choked on his drink. "What?" he sputtered.

"I was reading medical textbooks. Man inserts penis, woman gets pregnant, has baby. It was all very straightforward. I had no grasp of what it really meant." I searched his face, wondering if he could understand me. "I had no idea of the societal issues and the moral issues. It was all just biology, like with any mammal."

"So when you met Bobby you didn't worry about that?"

I twirled the cocktail straw, struggling to find the right words. "Bobby was the first outsider I met. I assumed that when a man and woman—or a boy and girl in our case—when they met and liked each other, they had sex. I had no other concept of a friendship or relationship other than a sexual one. Dr. Thell told me that's what men wanted and I should be cautious around any man." I shrugged. "I thought I was being cautious. I did what Bobby asked and hid his visits from her. I just had no idea of how to act around him other than how he wanted me to act."

"He took advantage of you," Nick muttered.

"From what I've heard, he did the same thing with

several other young women. I don't think I was the first. I was just probably the easiest because I had no idea of right and wrong. At least, right and wrong the way society defines it." I drew in a long breath, an old habit I'd cultivated to help me sort through my emotions and discover what was truly troubling me. "Wil was careful to show me what society thought I should do, but she also encouraged me to not worry about those so-called rules. She wanted me to know what I might encounter if I didn't follow those rules. It was a delicate balancing act for her. I didn't appreciate it when I was young, but looking back on it now, I see how tough it really was."

"I'm sorry, Jessa. I know this isn't how you wanted the trip to be. It's hard enough to face her death, but to have another family demanding that you acknowledge them just adds to the complexity."

"I don't want another family. I don't care how much money is involved." I took another sip and that's when my exhaustion hit me. The stress of traveling, the confrontation with Stephanie Bose, the constant background thoughts about Wil all combined at once.

Nick saw it immediately. "Let's go upstairs," he said. "Our food will be coming soon. I ordered a bottle of wine to go with it. We'll relax, eat something, then watch some television. Forget about all this."

I smiled weakly. "That sounds like a plan." I stood and waited for Nick while he went to the bartender, leaning over the partition and talking to him. Then we went to the elevator to the third floor. I went into my bedroom and kicked off my shoes, sliding into my old bunny slippers. When I came out, the food was arriving on a small cart. The waiter set everything on the table near the windows and left after holding out the chair for me.

I sat down and inhaled the aroma of roast chicken, potatoes, and asparagus. My stomach rumbled in appreciation and we dug into the food. I felt better for the mundane task of eating. It somehow put things in perspective for me.

"And here's the spun gold that was promised." When we finished our meal, Nick reached under the cart and carefully removed the desserts. One was a small square of crème brûlée with an artfully spun-sugar "tornado" on top. The other was a dish of ice cream with raspberries and a spun-sugar garland of small flowers encircling the dish.

"They're too pretty to eat." I turned each plate so I could view the delicate filagree from all angles. Nick watched me, smiling. "What?" I asked.

"I'm glad to see you relax a bit. This has been a tough trip for you."

"I didn't realize it was so obvious." I took a small bite of the ice cream, savoring the crisp flavor. "This is dessert artistry, isn't it?"

"My mother thought it was magical. Her words, not mine." He took a tiny bite of the crème brûlée.

"You're close to her, aren't you?"

He nodded. "We had some rough years when my father died. Then when she married my stepfather, it was rough for her because I was an idiot and treated her like she betrayed my dad and me. She was a beautiful woman. I can see why my stepfather was attracted to her. He liked beautiful things." Nick smiled wryly. "He liked to show her off to all his friends."

"But from the way you talked before, she still maintained at least some of her own independence. You said she did things that he didn't like." I pushed the ice cream toward him and sneaked a bite of the custard, which was like ambrosia. These desserts really were magical.

"Well, some of it she kept sort of private between her and me. And I think sometimes she did other things just to piss off my stepfather and stepbrother."

"What kind of things?" I leaned back in the chair, savoring my glass of red wine.

"Oh, like at Christmas time. She loved those Christmas crackers with corny jokes inside. You know the kind I mean?"

I shook my head. "I didn't celebrate Christmas until I went to live with Wil and Jake. They didn't have crackers."

"They're these little hollow tubes. Inside are cheap toys or candy or slips of paper with jokes. Like fortune cookies for Christmas."

"And your stepfather didn't like that?"

"He thought it was unsophisticated." Nick leaned back, too, smiling. "That's why she did it. Because it didn't fit in with his country club mentality. But he just acted country club. He didn't have any real class."

"Odd, isn't it? Family has so much to do with how we perceive the world. I think I see that more than some people do because I didn't have any family to influence me. You said once that your stepfather didn't approve of your career choice."

Nick took another bite of ice cream, his face hidden from me while he studied the sugar sculpture. The lighting was low in the room, putting most of his expression into shadow and highlighting his cheeks, giving him a gaunt appearance. "I had a lot of problems with my stepfamily. My stepbrother wasn't a good man, but his father didn't see it. His father thought the sun rose and set in his son."

"I suppose most parents feel that way." I saw the tense line of his shoulders and the way he seemed to hunch. Whatever relationship he had with his stepfather and stepbrother, it was obviously a troubling one. "You said your stepfather died. Are you in touch with your stepbrother?"

"No. We had a disagreement. We haven't spoken in decades." Nick raised his head, his eyes bleak. "It's an ugly story."

His tone of voice clearly said he didn't want to share the details. "I guess families can be complicated. I wouldn't know about that." I pushed away from the table. "That was an excellent meal. I could almost thank that woman for forcing us to eat here. I enjoyed it."

"I'm glad. I'm sorry she bothered us."

"How did she know where I was staying?" I took my glass of wine and went to the window to look out at the small town down the hill. "I feel like every time I turn around, that family is looking at me."

"Miller is a rich and powerful man in this part of the world. He probably has people on his payroll who can find out a lot of details about anyone." Nick joined me to stare at the lights below.

"I suppose I should know something about them since they're intruding on my life." I went to the couch and sank down. "Do you have any details?"

Nick picked up the wine bottle from the table and poured some for me, then emptied the bottle into his own glass. He sat in the armchair near me, his legs stretched out. "Wil had me do a lot of research when she found out they were asking about you. August Miller's family was in the shipping business. When he was in his early twenties, he and Cindy Gardener ran off together. Her family was in the lumber business. They probably knew each other because their families were in the same social circle."

"Cindy," I murmured. "No one ever mentioned her name."

"I've seen pictures of her. You do look a lot like her," Nick said. "She was so young and beautiful. Slender and small with hair just like yours, that odd white-gold color."

I shook my head, letting my hair slide over my shoulders. "It's saved me a lot in beautician fees—that's for sure. I never had to color it."

He smiled. "It would be a shame if you did. Anyway, August and Cindy ran off and got married. Miller's family blamed her for hooking him on drugs, but who knows who did what to who? The bottom line is, she developed a really bad drug habit after she gave birth. I read the files. It was probably caused by post-partum depression. Plus they had been cut off from the family money and were living in poverty. Neither of them knew how to fend for themselves. And they certainly didn't know how to care for a baby."

"Poor little rich kids out on the street?" I regarded him skeptically. "They gave up everything for love?"

He frowned. "Yeah, maybe they did."

I sipped my wine to hide my disbelief.

"Miller was afraid she'd die if he didn't get her what she needed. Somehow Professor Thell found them. She gave him the drugs he wanted. He gave her the baby. But Cindy Miller was too far gone. A month later she died.

He almost died, too, from a combination of drugs and malnutrition. When his family found him, they sent him to a rehab facility in Switzerland. It took a year for him to kick the habit and start to think rationally again. Stephanie Bose was right. He said he did try to find the baby, but he hit a dead end no matter where he looked. In the end, he took a job in his family business and lived in Europe for more than twenty years, working in their offices there."

"So when I was found, he didn't know about it? He didn't see the stories? What about his family? Wouldn't someone put two and two together?"

"I don't know. From what Wil told me, his family was very straight-laced, very conservative. It's possible they didn't want a child who was raised the way you were raised. And there was nothing to tie you to them. Thell died and never revealed who gave her the child. I'm not sure she even knew for certain."

I kept my opinion to myself. I was almost certain Thell knew exactly who my parents had been. I had no idea why she didn't reveal it, though.

"Miller came back to the United States after decades abroad. He was sixty by then and looking at retirement. He married Stephanie Bose, who was thirty at the time."

"And they have children?"

"She had children. Two kids. Richard is thirty-three now and a state senator. Wanda is thirty-one. Stephanie's first husband died in a car accident when they were little. She worked for Miller's company and that's how they met. There's talk that Richard might be groomed for the U.S. presidency."

"Really? Groomed by who?"

"One of those super PAC things. Richard Bose has

some real money at his disposal. He's home from Washington on holiday break and making the circuit, making sure he's seen at all the right functions."

"It sounds like you don't like him."

Nick sipped his wine, frowning. "I find it hard to trust him. I suppose it's because he's a politician, but it's also because he's too…" He stared into space, obviously searching for the right words. "He's too squeaky clean. Too Christian. I don't trust people who talk about being Christians and doing the right thing. Then they turn around and treat illegal immigrants like they're animals. Or they push their anti-abortion agenda and pretend it's for the good of the baby, but what about the woman who didn't want to have that child? People like that scare me because they're so sure they're right, and they want everybody to follow their rules."

"That sounds dangerously liberal," I said teasingly.

"America was founded on freedom of choice. Richard Bose is the kind of conservative who wants to limit options. He's well liked and well-funded, and that scares me, too."

I had nothing to say to that. It scared me, too. "I wonder why she is so anxious to find the daughter," I said, thinking out loud.

"Maybe she loves her husband, and she wants him to find what he's looking for."

"And maybe I'm skeptical and find that hard to believe." I yawned then smiled apologetically. "I'm sorry. Everything is catching up to me."

"I'm not surprised. It's been a whirlwind few days." Nick stood and held out his hand. I put mine in his, and he helped me to my feet. "Don't rush into any decisions about getting your hair tested," he said softly. "There's a lot riding on what you might find."

"I don't need the money." I stepped back but he still held my hand, keeping me in place.

"It's not so much the money. It's your past, your family. It might give you some closure to know where you come from."

"I've gotten along without them this long. Why have them now?" I gently wiggled my hand free and moved past him.

"Jessa."

I turned.

Nick brushed a kiss on my cheek. "Sleep well."

I nodded, surprised by his gesture, then crossed the room to my bedroom. I slipped inside and closed the door behind me. I debated locking it and decided against it. I doubted if Nick was in an amorous frame of mind. His kiss had been more consoling than seductive.

I shed my clothes and pulled on my sleep T-shirt, then plugged my phone in to charge next to the bed. I swallowed an OTC sleep capsule, then thoroughly washed my face, breathing a sigh of relief when I finally slid into the crisp bedding. All I would need was a few minutes of inane television shows, and I'd be out like a light.

As though challenging this assumption, my phone thumped on the bedside table. I glanced at the display. It was the same phone number that had been contacting me off and on throughout the day. My finger hovered over the *ignore* button but whoever was calling was persistent. I didn't want any calls interrupting me tomorrow when I was with Jake, so I answered. "This is Jessa."

"Oh, good, you're finally available. My name is

Wanda Bose. I need to talk with you."

"I'm sorry, I don't know anyone by that name." I lowered the phone but the voice squawked so loudly I raised it again.

"You talked to my mother this evening. Stephanie Bose?"

Ah. The rude woman in the restaurant, my supposed stepmother. "I have nothing to say to her or to you."

"Wait! Just hold on a minute. We need to talk in private." This woman sounded far more conciliatory than her mother and also much younger. There was almost a teenager-like quality to her phrasing and tempo.

"Why? We don't have anything to discuss."

"Yes, we do. My mother botched this up big time. If you and I can just talk, I know I can make you see reason. We can fix this. I know we can."

I held onto my patience but it was a challenge. "There is no this to fix."

"There could be," she insisted. "That's what we need to discuss."

"I keep trying to tell you. You will not get a sample of my hair. I don't care about the money."

"Awesome. That works for me. Let's talk."

What was it with these people? Why wouldn't they take no for an answer? "I'm here for a funeral. I don't know if I'll have time."

"Oh. I'm sorry," she said perfunctorily. Her lack of true empathy was almost insulting. "How about tomorrow?"

Good Lord. Was she insane? "That's impossible."

"Come on. Just a few minutes. That's all I need. I'm sure if we can talk face-to-face you'll understand why it's so important. My brother's future may depend on it."

I don't know your brother, and I don't care about him. I almost said it out loud. "I may have some time on Sunday," I said.

"Hmm. I have riding lessons Sunday morning and we're having a fund-raiser Sunday evening. How about the afternoon?"

I almost hung up. "I'm not sure what my plans will be. I'll call you tomorrow and let you know."

"I'll be busy most of the day."

"Then I'll leave a message. Good-bye." I ended the call and immediately turned off my phone. What an arrogant bitch. I used the remote to turn on the TV and cuddled back into my covers, propping enough pillows behind me so I could see. I watched a cop show with a predictable outcome then flipped through the channels, finally landing on the local news, which was just getting underway.

They opened with a story about a shooting in downtown Portland, then shifted to a reporter standing in front of a large building that was lit by various spotlights behind her. "State Senator Richard Bose, home from Washington during the Congressional break, spoke to civic leaders together regarding the uptick in violent crimes recently."

The scene shifted to a filmed segment, taken inside a spacious hallway crowded with people, most of them men in suits. The camera focused on one man in front. He appeared to be medium height with thick brown hair and prep-school handsomeness, his gaze fixed on several other men around him. "The recent pandemic caused an incredible amount of hardship for our working class. The Band-Aid handouts from the liberal government are not helping."

I saw immediately why Nick didn't like him. What would someone like Bose know about being working class? Everything about him screamed upper-crust elitist. He tried to dispel that image with his next words. "I've spoken with many people who are struggling to make ends meet, parents who have to juggle in-home schooling with jobs and elderly people who have to return to the workforce because they can't make ends meet. I sympathize with their plight. That's why we've seen this surge in crime lately. People are desperate and desperate people do desperate things."

"What an idiot." I glared at the glib politician spouting all the latest conservative nonsense.

"The only long-term solution to the problem of economic loss is the creation of more jobs. In order to do that, we need to provide stimulus to big business so they can put that money to use for everyone. The more tax incentives we give to large corporations, the more money will be available for job creation and job security."

A murmur of agreement and head nods greeted his words. "Bullshit trickle-down economics," I muttered. "It didn't work for Reagan and it didn't work for Trump. Wake up and join the twenty-first century. This isn't medieval England. The head of the company doesn't give a shit about the workers."

The camera cut back to the reporter. "Senator Bose will be speaking at a fundraiser on Sunday evening at the Midland Hotel in downtown Portland. The one-hundred-dollar-a-plate event is sold out, and we've been told there is a waiting list of people who wish to attend. The senator's campaign staff indicated that a portion of the proceeds would be donated to local food-shelf organizations."

"Yeah, right." I switched the channel and landed on a movie, a remake of one of the old classics. I settled back for some serious critiquing, but my mind kept going back to Richard Bose. If what people thought was true, that man was my stepbrother. I had two stepsiblings and a stepmother.

I remembered Nick's talk about his stepfamily. I had the distinct feeling that if it were proved that I was August Miller's child, the Bose family would want nothing to do with me. I would not fit in with them, their friends, or their political leanings. What about my so-called father? How did he feel about his stepchildren? He was in his late eighties now and had been a wild child once, or so it sounded like. What did he think of his stepson?

Perhaps more to the point, why was he trying to find me now? Was this truly just some old man's worry about facing death with my betrayal on his conscience? That's how I viewed it. My abandonment had been a betrayal. I was a child, a baby, and I was handed over to another person like a commodity to be bought and sold. And sell me he did, for drugs.

I yawned, the sleeping pill finally taking hold. It didn't matter. None of it mattered now. That was decades in the past. Those people were not my family. Jake and Wil were my family. I needed to focus on Jake and helping him. I needed to focus on Wil and my memories of her.

I fell asleep and thankfully had no dreams, or at least none that I remembered. I woke later than usual, almost seven-thirty, which was nine-thirty Midwest time. I guess I needed the sleep. I showered, then dressed in my funeral clothing of dark pants, a pale gray argyle sweater with black diamonds, and black flats. I swept my hair up into a French twist and regarded myself in the mirror.

"Time to say goodbye," I whispered.

I turned on my phone, then tucked it and a handkerchief into the small handbag I brought with me. I peeked out of the bedroom and found Nick sitting in the living area, the television on with the sound turned off. Last night's dishes and the cart were gone. He wore a dark gray shirt with dark tie and black dress pants. A gray suit coat was tossed over the armchair.

"Did you sleep okay?" he asked when he saw me.

"Yep, just fine."

"I heard from Jake," Nick said. "He asked if we'd come over. Some of his family are in town for the service, and they want to go out for brunch. He wanted us to come to the house so we could talk before joining them. The public service starts at two o'clock. We need to be at the funeral home by one o'clock. He wants to meet the rest of the family in an hour or so."

"Did he call me?" I dug into my purse and looked at the display of my cell phone. "I had my phone off. Wanda Bose called me, and I was afraid she'd call back."

"What did she want?"

"She wants to talk to me." I checked my call list and saw one from Jake an hour earlier. There was no voice mail, though, so I supposed he called Nick when he couldn't get in touch with me. I went to the window. There was rain mixed with snow falling, the dark and low clouds almost hiding the sight of the town below. The perfect day for a funeral, I thought.

"When?" His voice was so sharp I turned, surprised.

"When what?"

"When did Wanda Bose call you?"

"Last night before I went to bed. She wants to meet me. More of the bullshit about this inheritance, I suppose."

"Did you make plans to meet her?" Nick leaned forward, staring intently at me.

"No. I told her I'd call her once I know what my schedule is. Why? Do you think I should see her?"

"I think we should talk to Jake before you talk to anyone in that family." Nick stood. "Do you want to go?"

I glanced at the clock. It was almost nine. "Did he say what time?"

"He said to come over whenever you're ready. We can drive around town if you want to, so you can see what's changed. I know you haven't been back here for a while."

"I don't have many memories," I said. "I lived in that tower, then I moved in with Wil and Jake. I didn't really have a social life here."

"Then let's go see Jake." Nick seemed anxious, and I caught some of his nervousness.

"Sure." I got my coat and we left the suite. "What does he need to talk to me about? What's going on with this inheritance?"

Nick tapped the elevator button. "It's best if he tells you. It's time you know the truth."

Chapter 7

"That sounds ominous." I smiled, but Nick didn't seem to notice. He appeared tense and upset. "What's going on?"

The elevator arrived and he stepped inside, then gestured me to follow him. "There's more to this whole inheritance stuff than you know. Jake has the full story. It's best if he tells you about it."

I handed him my handbag, then pulled on my coat. "I figured there was something going on. Why can't you tell me?"

"Because he wants to."

I held out my hand and Nick passed over my bag, which I settled cross-body style. "Why are you involved in all this?"

He tensed. "What do you mean?"

"Wil said that she asked you to help because you were involved in my original case when I was found. Is that all it is?"

"I'm not sure what you're asking."

"Is Jake paying you?"

"Why does that matter?"

"Because if he isn't, then you must have some really good reason for dropping what you were doing, flying out to Iowa to babysit me, then flying back here and babysitting me some more." I kept my eyes focused on him and saw the faint flush in his cheeks when he avoided meeting my gaze.

"I told you. There wasn't a lot of dropping to do. I'm retired. I just putter around in my workshop and play golf."

The elevator doors opened and I started to step out. Nick beat me to it, leaving the car and glancing around the lobby. "What are you doing?" I demanded.

"Babysitting." We crossed the lobby, empty except for a man and woman sitting near the coffee bar, watching television. "Do you want some coffee? They have a continental breakfast. Juice, muffins and rolls." Nick paused.

"I can wait." I kept walking, and he hurried to catch up to me. I glanced at the check-in desk and nodded to the woman on duty, then left the building, for once exiting ahead of Nick.

"Hold on." He grabbed my arm and pulled me to a stop. "It's my job to make sure you're safe. That's hard to do if you're six steps ahead of me."

"Then keep up." I shook my arm free, not sure why I was so peeved. Maybe it was his babysitting comment. I fell into step with him, going to his car in the parking lot.

"Maybe you're hangry."

I shot him a glare. "I'm not hungry and I'm not angry. I'm peeved."

"That's hangry. Jake said he'd have some snacks ready when we got there." Nick unlocked the car doors and opened the passenger side door for me. "He said he remembered how you got when you had low energy."

"What do you mean, he knew—?" The door slammed and my question was cut short. I snapped on the seatbelt and leaned back, determined to try to regain my focus for the day. I had to help Jake through the ordeal ahead.

Nick slid into the driver's seat. "Are you sure you don't want to do a drive-around and see the town?"

"Whatever you want to do. I don't know how much time Jake needs to divulge his big secret." I smiled briefly at him, then returned my attention to the gray world outside my window.

Nick drove out of the parking lot and made a right turn, heading toward town. "Maybe we'll just drive around a bit until you feel better."

"I'm fine."

"Hmm." We drove through the small downtown. "That clothing store just came in last year. The storefront was empty for almost a year."

I nodded my acknowledgement of his comment.

"That ice cream shop has been there forever, I think."

I remembered the ice cream store. Jake said it wasn't as good as the one off the highway, but Wil and I stopped in now and then. We continued driving, Nick making comments here and there. After about twenty minutes, he turned around and we headed toward Jake's house. I hated to admit it, but I was glad we had taken the little tour around town. I felt much calmer and readier to deal with what was ahead.

So Jake was going to have snacks. I smiled. I remembered "snacking" with them. It was so casual, so relaxed. Wil would pull out some summer sausage, cheese, a few grapes, some crusty bread, and we'd slice what we wanted.

I'd been taught that meals were consumed at specific times of day. They always involved preparation, cooking, serving, and cleaning up. Wil and Jake ate when they were hungry, often on the patio with plates balanced on our laps. Cleaning up was done with laughter and jokes. It was a revelation to me. It was a revelation on top of the revelation that was the entire world.

We turned onto Tower Terrace Road, driving past the old dairy on the left side. It was no longer just a dairy but was now a retail store with big plate glass windows and a patio on the side that probably saw a lot of business in the summertime.

"They don't sell ice cream anymore," Nick said. "It's a brewpub."

"Oh, that's too bad," I said. "They had the best chocolate ripple ice cream."

"Their beer's pretty good, so I guess that's some consolation."

The road was paved now. When I lived here, it was gravel. There were other houses on either side, each set back from the road on large lots, probably all acreages. "It's grown up around here."

"Yeah, this subdivision took off about ten years ago. How long has it been since you visited?"

"At least that long. Wil and Jake came out to Minnesota a few times, and they've been to Iowa to visit. But I never enjoyed coming back here." I touched the window, rubbing away some of the fog. "It wasn't pleasant for me no matter how they tried. I just couldn't forget what had happened."

"What happened to you was a crime in more ways than one," Nick said.

I glanced at him. "It only took one crime to set my life on an odd path."

He met my eyes and nodded.

I leaned forward anxiously when he made a left turn into the long, winding drive. The house was like I remembered it, two stories with two windows top and bottom on either side of a center door. It was painted a pale blue now with navy trim. When I lived there, it was a pale yellow with green trim. It wasn't a big house but had ample room for the three of us. Just behind the house was the "barn," painted to match the house. It was really a two-car garage with an attic that I used as an artist studio during my artsy phase. Behind it was a stand of trees separating the property from a farm field.

I saw a couple of cats peeking out from the barn. "Jake and Wil always had barn cats," I said. "I wonder who's there now? The last time I was here they had three of them."

"I think there's four. Wil mentioned that the last time I was out here. She said it was a mother and some kittens that they got from the foster group in town."

"Look. The tree is still there. I helped plant that tree when I was first found and came to stay with Wil and Jake." The big pine tree almost filled the entire front yard.

"How big was it when you planted it?" Nick asked.

"About a foot tall. Jake made fun of us and said it would never amount to anything." I got out of the car and regarded the monstrous tree. "Look at it now."

Jake opened the front door and came out onto the stoop. "Punzi, thank you for coming." He was outlined by the lights from the hallway behind him, his dark pants and shirt blending in with shadows so he seemed to float.

I ran to him and was enfolded in a hug. Jake wasn't a big man, just five-eight or so, but he was wiry and strong. His hair, white now, was brushed back from his tanned face ,and he exuded an air of strength and youth despite his seventy years. I had a hard time imagining him as elderly, although I supposed it would happen sometime.

I let myself relax into his embrace. He was the only family I had, really. Jake and Wil taught me how to be a part of society. While Dr. Thell had technically raised me, it was Wil and Jake who taught me how to be a human in the modern world.

Jake released me, but kept his arm around my shoulders. "It's so good to see you. How long's it been? Three years? Four?"

I nodded. "I can't believe the tree is still here. I used to love to sit out here and stare at the trees." I pointed to the woods in the distance. "My room in the tower overlooked a small garden in back, but beyond it, all I saw was the back of a building."

"The warehouse," Nick said. "Your house was on the edge of the commercial district."

"How did you know?" Then I remembered. "Sure, you would know, wouldn't you? Was that your regular beat back then? Is that why you were there that night?"

He looked startled or maybe flustered. "I was new and didn't have a regular beat. I was in the right place at the right time."

"We're lucky you were," Jake said. "I wish the same could have happened for Wil." His voice wavered on her name.

I put my arm around his waist and we moved through the front door. "I can't believe she's gone. Do the police have any suspects? Any leads?"

"Let's get something to snack on and we'll talk." Jake looked over his shoulder. "Any problems getting here?"

"All okay," Nick said behind us.

"You act like somebody might try to snatch me or something." I gave Jake a nudge and went ahead of him into the kitchen, a large open room facing the old barn. The family room opened immediately off the kitchen through an arched opening. It was much the same, although there was newer furniture. It had the same configuration—two recliners and a small sofa—but they were new fabric and styles. The kitchen was also updated since I was there last. Now they had granite countertops instead of the laminate and stainless-steel appliances.

The old cutting board was still in its spot on the counter, though. It was shaped like a lumpy apple, chipped and gouged. I bought it for them when I received my first check from the university. It was the first time I ever shopped by myself, with my own money. I was almost eighteen years old. I wanted to repay Wil and Jake and the cutting board caught my eye at the downtown gift shop, looking so clean and new. The shopkeeper assured me it was an excellent thank you gift and I bought it on impulse. Wil treasured that old thing and had it sanded several times to bring fresh life to the wood.

I touched the board. "You still have it." I took off my coat, draping it and my bag over one of the chairs at the kitchen island.

"It still works," Jake said. He went to the fridge and brought out a couple of apples and some cheese. "Get the crackers, would you?"

I turned to the cabinet and collided with Nick, who was reaching for the same door I was. We did one of those odd little two-steps, with each of us moving at the same moment. I finally took a step back. "It's all yours."

Nick got the cracker tin and set it on the kitchen island next to Jake, who was slicing apples on the cutting board. I got another knife and began slicing cheddar cheese, stacking it on the serving tray sitting nearby. "What's this all about, Jake? You guys act like I'm in danger. Is it because of Wil? Because of what happened to her?"

"That's partly it," Jake said. "Wil wasn't sure how much to tell you. I guess I have to decide now."

"Tell me what?"

"Do you want coffee? A Bloody Mary?" Jake went to the coffeemaker on the counter.

"Coffee, black. Tell me what?" I got a mug from the rack on the wall and joined him.

"Let's sit down, then we can talk. I've had a lot on my mind lately. I need a minute to just take a breath and enjoy having you here." He smiled wanly at me.

I bit back the words I'd been on the verge of saying and nodded. "Nick said your family was in town. Your sister?"

"Yep, crazy Sally is here and her husband. Luckily, she left the kids behind. And Wil's brother is here, too. The private service will be tomorrow with them. Today is the public one. Wil was well liked both in town and at the courthouse. There'll be a full house, I'm sure." Jake's hand wavered over the apple.

I took the knife from him. "Why don't you take the coffee into the family room? I'll finish up the snacks."

"Thanks, sweetie. I'm so tired. I haven't slept much in the last few days." He wandered away and stopped in front of a picture of him and Wil on the side table near an armchair in the family room. It was taken at Mt. Hood on one of their camping trips. "I'm going to scatter her ashes near our favorite spot," he said softly, touching the picture. Jake turned to regard me. "I'll show you where it is, so you can scatter me when the time comes."

I almost dropped the knife. "I hope that won't be for a few years."

Jake went to the fireplace and poked at the low fire there. "Yeah. A few years."

I glanced at Nick, who had paused on his way into the family room. He shook his head. "You'll have to show me that spot, too," he said, going to Jake. "I've camped around Hood a lot and haven't found a spot I love. What about you, Jessa? Are you a camper?"

"Me? Heavens, no. My idea of roughing it is a motel without Wi-Fi."

"I remember when I first explained a computer to you." Jake turned away from the fireplace to smile at me. "You thought it was magic."

"It seemed like magic. I wasn't allowed to watch television, much less use a computer. I thought you guys were so modern, so hip." I set the apples on the tray with the cheese and went into the family room. I put the food next to the cracker tin on the big ottoman that served as footrest and coffee table.

Jake took his chair, the recliner that was nearest the fireplace. I perched on the sofa, putting an apple wedge and cheese slice on a paper plate and handing it to him. "You need to eat," I said when he started to protest. "You'll be living on adrenaline for the next few days. Grab food when you can."

"You're right." He nibbled the apple, then set the plate on the end table next to him. "It's good to have you home, girl."

"I wish I could have come under other circumstances. Do they have any idea who did it, Jake? Any leads at all?"

"No. The cameras in the courthouse security system were disabled during the time of the shooting, so that won't help."

"How did they get a gun in? Don't they have scanners or metal detectors?"

Nick and Jake exchanged a look. "What?" I demanded.

"I have informants who told me that there was someone working on the inside." Jake nodded when he saw my astonished look.

"You mean in the courthouse?"

"Yep. All it would take is one guard to turn his back at the right moment."

"But don't they screen people who come in? I mean, don't you have to have a reason to be there, especially at night?"

"It's easy to fabricate a story. Hundreds of people go through the checkpoints every day. It's hard to stay vigilant." Jake shook his head.

I started to question this, then I saw the answer in his eyes. "Someone paid somebody off in order to get to her."

He nodded. "We think so. I'm not sure if we'll ever find out who, though. I'm glad you got here and you're safe. I was worried."

I looked at Nick, who stood near the fireplace. "Was I in any danger?"

"I don't think so. That driver at the airport was odd, but we weren't followed. Maybe it was just the Miller family being overly proactive."

Jake nodded. "I expected they might be pushy."

I looked from one to the other. "Obviously, you guys have been staying in touch. I'll ask you again, Nick. Are you on the payroll?"

"It doesn't matter," Jake said. "We needed help and Nick was available."

"Help with what?"

Jake leaned forward, arms resting on his thighs so his hands could dangle in front of him. I recognized that posture. This was Jake the Attorney, analyzing a client before accepting a case. I'd seen him and Wil talk in this room often, drinks next to them while they hashed over the events of the day. "One of my contacts told me you might be in danger."

I knew better than to ask who it was who said that. Jake could never divulge the identity of a source. "Why?"

"The inheritance."

"What inheritance? I haven't agreed to any DNA testing. Besides, the old man is still alive, right?" Jake nodded. "So it's moot. He could change his mind tomorrow and disinherit me. How did you hear this?"

"I have confidential informants working for me. They know about our past together, how Wil and I helped you." His voice wavered when he said her name. "They came to me."

I turned to Nick. "Why are you involved?"

"I asked him," Jake said. "He was involved in the original case, so he knew you. I wanted you to talk to someone you could trust."

"You're saying Wil's death had something to do with that inheritance."

"Maybe. She's been getting threats." Jake stopped,

blinking hard before correcting himself. "She was getting threats. The police are tracking down all leads. She worked on some high-profile cases. Judges have been targeted around the country by white supremacists."

I nodded. I'd read a story about that last week. It sounded plausible and I wanted to believe him. I didn't want to think I'd caused the death of a woman I considered a big sister and a mentor.

"You need to take this seriously. Nick is here to protect you, plus we have other people in place, keeping an eye on things."

A muted buzzing was loud in the quiet room. Nick pulled his phone out of his suit coat pocket. "I'm sorry. I need to take this call." He headed for the kitchen, his phone held to his ear.

I watched him leave, then turned to Jake. "I don't understand why he's here. Doesn't he have something better to do?"

"Nick has his reasons. Please don't pry. He'll tell you if and when he wants to. Just know that we have the support of law enforcement, and he's part of it. We don't have firm evidence, just the word of a low-life criminal implicating one of Portland's richest families."

"I still don't understand. I won't allow them to test me, so what does it matter?"

Jake jumped to his feet. "There's more to it than that. You need to trust me."

"I do trust you, but I don't understand. If I don't let them test my hair, then this all ends. I go home and the old man dies and the family inherits his money." Jake ran his hand through his hair, a stress gesture I recognized. "What is it? What aren't you telling me?"

"There are some very real legal implications around all of this. I didn't want to involve you, but you're getting involved despite our best intentions. Wil was worried this might happen."

"What might happen?"

Jake sat back down. "August Miller is elderly, and his wife is trying to have him declared mentally incompetent. She claims that his drug-addicted youth has impaired his ability to reason coherently. She wants total control of his estate."

"Okay," I said slowly. "What does that have to do with me?"

"His legal team is fighting it. Miller made a will that stipulated that only a blood relative could inherit that portion of his estate which was derived from his first wife's assets. She was an heiress. When she died, he inherited her estate, which at the time was quite substantial. He invested it, then went on to create his own wealth using his family's connections and money."

"So he's a millionaire twice over?"

"That's one way to consider it. He set up a fund for his first wife's portfolio. It can only be inherited by a blood relative—his lost daughter. If she isn't found, the estate reverts to a charity endowment to help drug addicts overcome their addictions."

"I thought he and Stephanie Bose had children?" I frowned, trying to remember the details.

"They're her children from a previous marriage." Jake raised his head to stare at me, his eyes red-rimmed and raw. "You may be his only heir."

I nodded slowly. "I can understand why he might want to find me. But why does she want to find me? Why does she want to prove that I'm his heir?"

"She wants to prove that you aren't."

"Isn't that a risk? What if I am?"

"Then she'll negotiate a settlement with you because otherwise you'll be tied up in court for years and probably never see any of the money."

"Well, shit." I looked around the room, struggling to make sense of what I was hearing. "What do you think? Is the old man crazy?"

"I don't know," he said. "I've only spoken with people around him, the people who aren't his family. His legal team has talked to me about it because they know about my involvement with you. They don't think he's incompetent at all. They think he's tied up the money so his stepchildren don't get their hands on it." Jake smiled faintly. "Apparently Mr. Miller doesn't approve of his stepson's conservative views and political ambitions."

"Yeah, I saw him on television. The stepson. Nick mentioned that he might be presidential material."

"Anyone can be presidential material," Jake said. "Whether they endure the process is another story. Bose has managed his political career very astutely. Plus he has some powerful backers and investors supporting his ambitions."

"I spoke to the stepdaughter, to Wanda Bose. She called me."

"What? When?" Jake looked at Nick when he re-entered the room. "Did you know that Wanda Bose called Jessa?"

"Yeah. Last night." Nick shot me a stern look. "The next time one of them calls you, please let me know immediately."

"Yes, Mother," I muttered.

"This is serious, Jessa." Jake's voice was so sharp

that I flinched. "One simple way for that family to solve their problem is to eliminate anyone who might be an heir. And right now, you're the only candidate. If you're out of the picture completely, there's a good chance Bose and her children could go to court and have Miller's will declared null and void, especially if they can find a sympathetic judge regarding Mr. Miller's competency. Have you considered that possibility?"

I looked from him to Nick then back to Jake. "You don't mean it, do you? People don't go around killing people because…" My voice trailed away when I saw the hard look in Nick's eyes. "What kind of money are we talking about? A million dollars? Two million?"

"August Miller is a billionaire," Jake said flatly. "He was listed on Forbes Top 100 Richest a few years ago. His net worth has taken a bit of a hit lately because of stock market fluctuations, but he's probably still worth at least twenty or thirty billion. Most of that is from his first wife's memorial fund. It's probably fifteen billion. The remainder is tied up in stocks from his company."

I gaped at him. "What?"

Jake nodded. "That's why you have to take this seriously."

"But—but—I can't be a billionaire. I don't know a damn thing about money like that. I can't inherit—I can't manage—I—" My brain couldn't process such a staggering thought. "I'm not a billionaire person, Jake."

"I told you he was wealthy," Nick said. "What did you think I meant?"

"I thought, you know, movie star wealthy, not Jeff Bezos wealthy," I snapped.

"I think you need to allow them to test your hair. We can find out, once and for all, if you're the child he's seeking. Miller has a hair sample from the baby, and there was a sample taken from you when you were found. Those two match. All you need to prove is that you're the girl from the tower. I'd testify to that and so would other people." Jake looked at Nick, who nodded. "That won't hold up in court, though. Only the hair sample will do it. All the facts point to it, but there's an outside chance it isn't you." When I started to speak, he continued, overriding me. "A very slim outside chance. If it isn't, then you're off the hook, and life goes back to normal."

"But what if I am?" I stood, anxious to move. "I can't be a billionaire, Jake. I'm not cut out to manage that kind of money." I paced in front of the fireplace, trying to sort out everything that was said.

"August Miller has a team of financial advisors who will work with you. And if you do inherit, you should consider making a settlement to Stephanie Bose. That might appease her enough to drop any legal action against you." Jake reached for my hand, pulling me to a stop. "I'm not going to sugarcoat this, Jessa. If you're proven to be August Miller's heir, the Bose family will pull out all the stops to see that you don't get the money. Your entire past will be dug up and dissected. Everything."

I stared down at him. "You told me my records were sealed."

"When there's this much money involved, records can get unsealed. It could get very ugly. You need to be prepared for that. If you can come to an agreement with the Bose family, it might be to your advantage."

I pulled away from him. "How long have you known about this? Why now?"

"Miller's people touched base with me in the summertime. That was when he started talking about changing his will."

I took a slice of apple from the tray and resumed pacing. "Why?"

"I don't know why. Maybe he's feeling his mortality. Why does it matter?"

I chewed thoughtfully, my mind still trying to grasp the notion that I had an opportunity to be Really Rich. "He's gone forty years without trying to find me. Now all of a sudden it's a critical need. I don't understand."

"Maybe it's his stepson," Nick said.

I spun around. I had forgotten he was even in the room. He sat at the far end of the couch, watching us. "What about the stepson?"

"He's considering a run for the presidency. Maybe his handlers are worried that if Miller's past is exposed, it might harm his stepson's chances. I've heard rumors that Miller and his stepson don't agree on a lot of political issues. Maybe this is Miller's way of throwing a wrench in his stepson's plans."

"I think the American people have proven very thoroughly that they don't care about the character of the man elected president," I snapped. "An old scandal from decades ago won't even be a blip on the media screen."

"Nick might have something," Jake said. "I got the impression that Miller's legal team is worried about the people backing Richard Bose. There's a lot of money from unknown donors supporting his candidacy. If Miller is declared incompetent, any scandal would cling to Miller, not to Bose."

"There must be some other reason. Or maybe there isn't. I don't know the man." I shook my head. "This is all crazy."

"I don't think it matters why," Jake said. "It's happened and we have to deal with it. I wanted you to be aware of everything that's at stake, Jessa. It's not just the money. It's the attention that will go along with it. I'm afraid it'll come out about your past. It's almost inevitable. If you inherit, your life will change completely."

"I understand. I guess it's lucky that I'm accustomed to my life being changed completely. But like I said before, this is all a moot point. Even if it's proven that I'm his daughter, Miller may change his mind." I glanced at the clock on the mantel. "We'd better go meet the relatives, Jake. You know how Aunt Sally gets when she has to wait on us."

He rose from the chair, using the arms to push himself up. "Until this is settled, it's important that you have security around you. Nick will stick with you. If he can't be nearby, we've arranged for other security people to be in place." Jake looped his arm through mine and we headed for the kitchen, Nick behind us.

"I'm still not sure I want to go through with this," I warned. "I don't want his money or his attention."

"Think about it. This might be the most important decision you make, Jessa. For better or worse, you're in the spotlight. I don't know if they'll be content to just let you walk away."

"I'm not going to worry about it for now," I said gently. "Today is all about Wil. I'll make a decision tomorrow about Miller."

Jake touched my cheek. "I'll support you no matter what." He looked past me to Nick and nodded.

I had the feeling there was more they weren't telling

me, and I was grateful for that. I had enough to worry about as it was.

More than enough.

Chapter 8

I rode with Jake to the restaurant where we were to meet his family, while Nick followed in his car. "The town has changed a lot," I commented, peering through the snowy fog at the houses we passed.

"We're part of Portland now. A lot of folks from there have moved out to Rampian because even with heavy traffic, we're only twenty or thirty minutes away from downtown."

"Nick said only Midwesterners counted distance using time. I'll have to tell him you do it, too." I glanced at the rear-view mirror, spying Nick's car several cars behind us.

"Did you remember him? Were you surprised when he came to see you?"

"Surprised? I was stunned. I thought I'd left my past far behind me. And I didn't recognize him at first. It wasn't until I saw his eyes that I knew who he was. It's been so long ago. He was so young when I first saw him. I never saw him again after that day. Well, just once, for a second or two."

"Nick took a lot of heat for testifying at the trial." Jake checked the mirror, verifying the subject of our conversation was still behind us. "He was a first-year cop. The prosecutor did a shitty job of prepping him for what he'd have to face."

"You mean because Bobby was the son of one of the

richest men in town?" I asked.

"And because the prosecutor was probably getting kickbacks from Reagan's father. I think Nick was shocked to find out the legal system was rigged. I always wondered why he was surprised, given his background. But maybe his mother protected him from knowing too much. Wil talked to her a few times and that's what it sounded like." Jake glanced at me. "Nick's a good guy. When he moved back here, he touched base with me. It would have been tricky for him to work on the Rampian PD, so I helped him get set up for private work."

"Why was that a problem? Because of his stepfather? Because of the trial?"

Jake's dark brown eyes widened with surprise. "You know about his family? His stepfather?"

"I know that he has a stepfather and a stepbrother. I know he had a tenuous relationship with them and he no longer stays in contact with his stepbrother." I smiled wryly. "Just think, I could have a similar relationship with the Bose family if it turns out I'm August Miller's kid."

"I just can't imagine you and Richard Bose having much in common," Jake said. "You'd have about as much in common as Nick does with his stepbrother. Nothing."

"You know the stepbrother?"

"I've had dealings with the family." The distasteful way he said it spoke volumes about Nick's stepfamily. "Although I haven't had anything to do with them for years. The father died and the son moved away. The town is better off without them." Jake fell silent, glaring at the road ahead.

"Where's today's service?" I asked when he drove

out of Rampian to the main road leading to Portland.

"The Willows. You remember it. That big funeral home place on the way into town. They have a large meeting hall that we thought would be useful. We have the visitation from one o'clock until four this afternoon. Then we'll have the private service tomorrow for the family in late morning." His hands clenched the steering wheel, knuckles white. "I hope you'll stay until Monday at least. I'd like to have some time to spend with you without everybody around. We need to discuss this whole situation with your inheritance."

"I don't want that to distract from honoring Wil," I said. "That's the most important thing right now."

"I don't know if you ever knew this, but Wil and I couldn't have children. It was one of those odd quirks that both she and I had something wrong that prevented us from getting pregnant. When you came into our life, it was like being handed a child without all the diapers and the feedings." He reached out. I put my hand in his, giving it a squeeze.

"I was lucky to have you two there to catch me when I was tossed into the big world. I honestly had no idea how to navigate my way around society. Wil never once made me feel guilty because of what happened. She made me understand that it wasn't my fault. I was the victim not just of Dr. Thell, but of Bobby and how he took advantage of me. It wasn't until I'd been out in the world for a while that I realized how unusual that was."

Jake squeezed my hand. "Rape victims are often made to feel at fault. Wil saw this so often in her legal practice. And it was even more critical for you because you had no context for what happened. You were a blank slate. It was essential that you be allowed to come to an understanding of what he did without having all kinds of guilty connotations tossed in, too."

"It's so odd," I said. "There are times when I feel like it was just a day or two ago. And then it feels like it was so far away from me that it happened to someone else. I don't really blame him anymore. From what I know of him, it was all a part of who he was. I wasn't the first woman he used, but I hope I was the last."

"You weren't a woman. You were a child." Jake released my hand when we turned onto the freeway going into the city. "That was one of the key facts that Wil had to prove. You were vulnerable, and Reagan took advantage of that. It was a travesty. That's why I'm so worried about this whole inheritance thing. The rape, your pregnancy, your miscarriage. All of that might come out."

"I don't care," I said immediately. "It was forty years ago and it's all behind me. It's not an embarrassment. It's just a part of my history."

He was quiet for a moment then he asked, "Have you ever told anyone else about your past? About what happened to you?"

"No. I mean, I told Janice some of it because when Nick showed up, it all sort of came out. But I never told anyone about Bobby and all that."

"But you've never told a lover or someone close to you? You never told someone about it all, how you were abandoned by your parents? The miscarriage?"

I shook my head. "I never really got that close to anyone," I admitted. "There was never anyone I wanted to settle down with. I didn't think I needed to share it."

"I know Wil worried that perhaps you weren't healed the way we hoped. When you never found

128

someone to share your life with, we worried that maybe your past was affecting you."

"I suppose it did, but I'm happy, Jake. I like my life. I don't mind being alone. I've never felt that I've lacked for anything. You and Wil did the best you could. If there's any fault, it's on my part, not yours. I just haven't found anyone that I really wanted to share those details with."

We drove in silence for another few minutes. "It would be tough to explain your past to someone," Jake said. "It would be hard for a stranger to understand how totally innocent you were of the world."

"I'm not sure how much that affects my relationships now," I said. "It happened so long ago that it feels like it happened to another person." I stared out the window. "Until I come back here, I suppose. Then it brings it all back."

"I'm glad the house is gone, at least. You don't have to see that anymore. You don't have that to remind you."

"Nick said they built a school on the site and there are houses now all around it. It was so rundown before."

"Wil was one of the key players in getting that property condemned She worked hard on the neighborhood revitalization."

"Nobody knew about the details, right? My case and the location was never publicized. The story just said I was found in Oregon near Portland, right?"

"That's right. We kept media coverage to a minimum. Wil worked behind the scenes to make sure the area where the house stood was a target for change, nudging the city planning commission. We went out and watched on the day they tore down the house." Jake glanced at me. "I shot video of it. Wil had it transferred to a DVD. We were going to give it to you for a Christmas present this year."

I had a sudden memory of me standing at the window, staring down into the walled garden. There was a small path winding through the flowerbeds, herbs on my left and sunflowers on my right. Every spring, Thell would buy seeds. I'd start plants indoors under grow lights. Then I'd transplant them outside when the weather was warmer. "I've never had a garden again," I murmured. "I just now realized that. Even when I had a house with enough space for one, I never put in a garden. Maybe there are residual effects I'm not aware of."

"I think that's true of everyone. We all have things in our past that come back to haunt us now and then." He pulled into the parking lot of the Prince's Palace Restaurant. "Like my sister and her husband."

I laughed. "Sally isn't that bad."

"She's a pain in the ass," Jake said, shutting off the car. "But she's family, so I can't get rid of her. I'm glad I have you with me to counterbalance her effect." He slung an arm around my shoulders, and we went to the front door.

"Should we wait for Nick?" I looked back at the parking lot.

"He'll be along soon. I think he had some errands to run." Jake pulled open the door, and we went into the dark interior.

I hesitated, letting my eyes adjust to the low lighting. Jake moved ahead, waving to someone. I followed and was immediately engulfed in a hug. "Jessa, it's so good to see you, but what a crappy reason for it!"

My "aunt" Sally was a big woman, slightly taller than Jake and at least twice his width with ample everything—bosom, hips, and personality. Her husband, Marco Zapallo, was equally overwhelming. Jake called them the Large Loud Zapallos, an effect doubled when their five children joined in. Thankfully, the children and their children were absent today, which meant it was a relatively restrained affair.

Both Wil's relatives and Jake's had accepted me into the family when I went to live as a ward of the court with Wil and Jake. They were never told the complete details of what happened, but I think they intuited a lot about my past. I always viewed them as my family, too, and today was no exception.

I was drawn to the table where Marco was already seated next to Wil's brother, Karl. He was tall and slender, the same way Wil had been. He had the same dark hair and bright blue eyes that Wil had. Her picture was in the middle of the table. I picked it up to study while conversation swirled around me.

The picture showed Wil standing next to a tree, Mt. Hood in the background. She was smiling at the camera, her dark brown hair cut short and spikey around her head. The shorts and T-shirt she wore emphasized her slender figure and tanned body. Her energy seemed to radiate out from the photo.

I remembered the first time I saw her. I was in the hospital bed and she was in the chair next to me. There was a light on over her shoulder, which shone on the papers on her lap. She wore a business pantsuit, navy blue and tailored for her slim frame. I had seen pictures of young women in books, but Thell was the only woman I knew personally. Thell was older, in her late fifties, with gray hair cut into a severe bob and plain. She never wore makeup or did anything to enhance her appearance.

Wil was pretty and professional with makeup that enhanced her looks and a style that was a revelation to me. I had no idea a woman could be chic, professional, and pretty. When Wil sensed me watching her, she raised her head and smiled. "Hi, there. My name is Wil. I'm going to help you."

"Help me with what?" I asked.

Wil stood and came to the bedside, looking down at me. "I'm going to make sure you get well, then we'll find you a nice place to live."

"What about the tower? And the garden?" I looked around the room, at the unfamiliar furnishings and the machines next to the bed. "I need to take care of the garden."

She put her hand on my arm, and I stared at it in amazement. Her nails were painted a pretty pink color and her skin was smooth and unmarked. My own hands were rough from housework and gardening. "Who are you?" I whispered. "Are you my fairy godmother?"

Wil gently touched my forehead, pushing my hair back. "I'll try to be."

She had been like a fairy godmother, I realized now, setting the picture back on the table. Wil had carefully and cautiously taught me about life, people, society, and how to interact with others. I owed her and Jake everything, but I especially owed Wil, because she taught me how to be a woman.

I spent the next hour or two getting caught up with the relatives, exchanging stories about children and grandchildren, examining pictures, and sharing memories about Wil. Jake listened to us all, his gaze often going back to the photo on the table. I could only imagine his feelings. He and Wil had been together all their lives. They dated in college and got married while they were both in law school. I had never had that kind of closeness to another human being. For the first time I wondered what I was missing.

We ate a light lunch, then got back into cars and went to the funeral home which was just a few blocks away. The building had three large entry/exit doors. When we entered, we saw three large entryways, one directly ahead and the others off to the side, all corresponding to the outside doors. A placard was on an easel with Wil's picture near the entryway for the room on the left.

The funeral director came out and met Jake, leading him into that room. It was a large open space with chairs throughout in small groups, chairs at the far end of the room, and a podium near the back. On the wall immediately near the entryway was a table. It was covered with pictures of Wil, some framed and some loose.

"We'll have the video montage playing while people are here," the director said to Jake, leading him to the back of the room. "People will come into the room, pass the exhibit, then they can greet the family here and go on to mingle and chat if they prefer."

I paused by "the exhibit" to look at the pictures. "She was the leader in our family," Karl said softly, touching a picture of Wil when she was a child, sitting on a pony. "I remember one time she walked me home from school because one of the other kids was bullying me. She beat him up."

I laughed. "That sounds like Wil. She didn't take crap from anybody."

Karl looked at Jake, still in conversation with the

funeral director. "I'm glad you were able to come here to be with him. I hope you can stay for a few days. He needs people around him now."

"I'll stay if he needs me," I murmured. I spied Nick coming in the front door. "Excuse me." I hurried out to the lobby. "You missed lunch," I said.

"I needed to touch base with a couple of people. How's it going?"

"It's just getting started." I moved to one side when people came in the front door. A woman with the funeral home met them, handing over a small program and gesturing to the room where Jake and the family were standing. Jake glimpsed me and gestured. "I need to join him. Is everything okay?"

"I had to talk to representatives from the Miller legal team. They wanted to set up a time to take a hair sample."

I stopped in mid-step. "I'm not sure I want to do that. I thought I made that clear."

"You did. But they've contracted with a lab to do the specialized testing that's needed and that lab has a representative here in town. I told them that we would contact them tomorrow to let them know if or when you agree to the testing. If you agree to do it, they'll take the sample and will have the results within a few days."

"Jessa, you're needed inside." Karl touched my arm. "Jake wants you with us in the receiving line."

I moved away from Nick. "I'd like some time to think about this."

"The longer you wait, the more pressure they'll put on you."

I walked away, so angry I didn't dare speak. I was tired of it all, tired of people telling me what I should and shouldn't do, tired of worrying about money that may or may not be mine, tired of thinking about some old man who was drowning in his regrets at the end of his life. I joined Sally, Karl, and Jake, slipping into place on Jake's left side.

The next few hours passed in a blur of a never-ending line of people waiting to shake my hand, express condolences, and share an anecdote about Wil. Many were from the legal profession, but there were a surprising number of people who had been clients. They came from all walks of life, all financial backgrounds, and all layers of society. At one point, I asked Karl about it.

"She did a lot of pro bono work before she became a judge," he answered softly. "She and Jake both worked for Legal Aid in their spare time. A lot of the people came here for Jake and for her. He's well liked, too."

I kept an eye on Jake throughout the afternoon. He appeared tired but cheered by the turnout. Sally was watching him, too. At one point she had him sit down, diverting the people in line to join him in one of the chair groupings. She got him a glass of water and stayed nearby, deftly moving mourners along when it appeared he was wearying.

Nick stayed near the front of the room, watching the crowd. It was around three o'clock that I took a break, going to the restroom to splash water on my face and draining the water bottle one of the funeral home helpers handed me.

I came out of the small hallway where the restrooms were located and went to the front of the funeral home, standing near the exit doors to look at the gray and dreary day. It felt like we'd been trapped in a perpetual fog all day. Now that the sun was going down, it would finally be true darkness, not this gray mist.

"Hello, girly."

I froze. No one had called me that in forty years. I struggled to analyze what I felt. Shame, regret, fear, and more than anything—shock. I turned slowly.

A man stood near one of the other exit doors, mostly in the shadows. He was short and overweight, with thinning black hair. His dark suit made him blend into the fading twilight. When he stepped forward, I saw him clearly. He had an oval face, dark eyes, and a scar on his right cheek. I breathed a sigh of relief. It was a stranger. I didn't know him. "Who are you?"

"Oh, that hurts. You don't recognize me?" He took another step toward me. I instinctively took a step back. "You haven't changed. You're still beautiful. Your hair is shorter, though. It was so long before. I remember how it felt to have it falling around us."

I shook my head. "You can't be him. He moved away."

"I looked for you. They hid you away from me, though, and I couldn't find you." The man approached me. I once again stepped back, feeling the other exit door at my back. "I petitioned the court to find you, to explain what happened. It wasn't like they said, girly. I loved you then. I never meant to hurt you."

I couldn't breathe. My lungs were burning. I was certain I'd faint. "I don't know you."

He tilted his head to one side. "What says 'Oh, Oh, Oh'?"

I swallowed hard, fighting the bile that rose in my throat. "Santa walking backwards," I whispered.

"Why did the turkey join the band?" He moved forward.

136

I was frozen, unable to tear my gaze from his. "Because it had the drumsticks." He told me those jokes. I remember him saying how his little brother loved the corny jokes. I didn't understand some of them. He had to explain them to me.

"Now do you know me?"

I shook my head, more to try to shake the image of him away than to deny anything. "Why are you here?"

"I'm with a friend. She came to pay her respects." His voice was so bland it was almost insulting, like someone's death was of only passing interest. "I thought you'd be here. I know you cared about her." His gaze went past me to the picture of Wil on the placard outside the reception room. "I begged her to let me talk to you. I had to see you, had to explain."

I struggled to make sense of what he said. Wil had impressed on me that under no circumstances should I reply to anything I might receive from Bobby, back when it happened or into the future. And I hadn't received any word from him. I didn't love him. Or at least, at the time I didn't think I did. I was so naïve and so unsure about relationships, I had no idea what love was.

No, Bobby was just a contact with the outside world. I had read that boys and girls had sex so when he wanted to have sex, it made sense to me. It was pleasant, but he wasn't an adept lover, and he didn't care much for my enjoyment. I found that out years later, when I had other lovers who showed me what true reciprocity was.

I was so bewildered when I was rescued that I simply gave my deposition to the judge and never really gave him another thought. Wil told me that he'd be punished and I was not to blame for that. Bobby should have known better than to take advantage of me. Because of that, he was punished.

"It was a mistake," he said, startling me out of my memories. "They didn't know how I felt about you. I tried to explain, but then they put you into hiding. I didn't even know your real name. I couldn't find you." He looked and sounded so contrite, so confused.

"I didn't have a name," I murmured.

"I thought you were just joking with me." He moved closer. I could see the ridge along the scar on his cheek.

"What happened to you?" I didn't mean just the scar. I meant everything. When I knew him, Bobby Reagan had been slender and athletic, with thick wavy hair, laughing blue eyes, and a handsome face like the statues in my textbooks. The man in front of me had jowly cheeks, sunken eyes, a receding hairline and a distinctive paunch that made his suit coat look ill fitting.

"This?" He touched his cheek. "It was an accident."

I didn't believe that. The way he said it and the hard look in his eyes told me that it was something horrific, something that still ate at him. I looked past him and saw a man in the doorway to Wil's service, his gaze fixed on us. He was muscular appearing, his suit straining his shoulders. I didn't know him, but I'd seen him talking to Nick earlier. He must have seen something in my panicked stance because he moved toward me. "Is everything okay?" he asked. "Nick asked me to keep an eye on things. Are you okay?"

"I don't know," I said. "I didn't expect to—" I turned. "Where did he go?"

"The man with you?" I nodded. "He left by the side door. Do you need me to find him? He's probably outside." The man moved toward the exit.

"No, that's okay. It's not a problem." I saw Sally

beyond him, waving at me. "Excuse me." I hurried back into the reception hall. "What's up?"

"I think we need to get Jake out of here. He's had some heart issues in the past year. This is too much for him. We need to figure out a way to get him to leave. If I nag him about his health, he'll just dig in his heels."

I looked past her. Jake was seated among some people I didn't know. He did look exhausted and somehow frail. "Let me see what I can do. I think the crowd has thinned out. Maybe you can gather up anyone left and get them moving toward the door."

She nodded and bustled away. I approached Jake, smiling apologetically at the people with him while I leaned over to whisper, "I was wondering if we can head out soon. I'm still on Midwest time and I'm hitting the wall."

"I'm tired, too," he admitted. "I'll just say good-bye to a few folks, then we can leave."

I patted his shoulder and straightened. I spied Nick and the man from earlier talking near the doorway. When Nick saw me watching them, he nodded, then headed straight across the room for me. I intercepted him halfway. "Jake is getting tired and we need to go," I said in a low voice. "Sally is worried about him and so am I."

Nick looked over my head, then nodded. "I'll drive you two home. Hold on while I make arrangements to have my car dropped off at the house." He started to turn away, then paused. "Who were you talking to earlier? Bill said you looked upset."

"No, it was fine." The last thing I wanted was a lecture about talking to a ghost from my past. That would really get Jake upset. "Just someone with condolences. I'll go get Jake moving toward the door."

I think Sally must have done her job well because we were able to leave the reception area in another twenty minutes. Nick took Jake's car keys, and soon we were driving through the sleety rain. "I'm pleased so many people came out for Wil," Jake said. He sat in the front seat with Nick, and I was in the back, staring out the window.

"Two hundred people," Nick said. "That's what the funeral director said. They counted up the people from the guest book."

I couldn't believe it was actually Bobby. I kept replaying the conversation in my head. What had happened to him? He'd been in jail, but only briefly, or that's what I was told. Forty years. Did forty years really make that much difference in our appearance? I looked at my reflection in the window and realized that yes, it did make that much difference.

"...in for a drink, won't you?" Jake had turned on the seat and was looking at me.

"What?"

"You two will come in for a drink, won't you? Karl is staying at the house tonight. We talked about getting a pizza."

I glanced at Nick. "Sure, we can come in for a minute or two. I'm beat, though. I think I'll make it an early night."

Jake smiled. "That sounds good to me, too." He turned back around.

Should I tell Jake or Nick about talking to Bobby? What good would that do? I couldn't tell Jake, I knew that. He had too much to deal with now anyway. No, and if I told Nick, he'd probably get upset and maybe he'd tell Jake. Or would they be upset? What did it matter?

I thought Bobby had moved away. What was he doing there? Did he really try to find me or was that just some bullshit story? The more I considered it, the more I decided it was probably a lie. He had done nothing but lie to me the entire time I knew him. Why would he change now?

"Hey, Nick," Jake said. "I think we should pull in here."

"What?" Nick glanced at him. "Where?"

"Over there. I think we should pull in over there." Jake pointed to the right side of the road. "That exit, there. Take it."

"What's going on?" I strained forward to peer between the seats. Through the drizzly rain I saw the exit sign. Beyond it I saw a blue information sign. *Northwest Regional Hospital, this exit.* "Jake, what's happening? Are you okay?"

He looked back at me. "No, I'm not. We need to go there. Now."

I unhooked my seat belt and leaned over the seat to look at him. Jake's face looked pasty pale and sweat glistened on his forehead. I reached for his hand and he grabbed mine. "I'm not feeling so good, Punzi."

"Not to worry," I whispered. "We'll take care of it."

Nick glanced at me and nodded. "On our way."

Chapter 9

"At least it wasn't a heart attack." I sipped from a bottle of water, exhaustion making my hand tremble.

Nick and I sat at a table near the entryway in the hospital cafeteria. Two other tables held visitors. One table looked like hospital personnel in scrubs. The four men all looked tired, but it was almost midnight, so I suppose that made sense. The other table held an older man and woman. They both seemed exhausted and beyond speech, each of them concentrating on the tea in the paper cups in front of them. I wondered what tragedy they had just come from.

"It was a near thing, though." Nick sat across from me, his unusual eyes brightly lit by the overhead lights. "I'm glad the hospital was so near."

"That was luck." I shivered, remembering the controlled panic when Nick left the freeway, careening into the emergency room parking lot of the area hospital. I was on my mobile phone, frantically calling Sally and Karl to let them know we would not be at the house and to have them meet us at the hospital.

Two hours later, we were all crowded into Jake's tiny emergency room, a semi-private space that strained at the seams to accommodate us. "You're under a lot of stress and from your records, it appears you've been under stress for the last few months," the doctor said sternly.

"We can't do much about that," Sally said. "We have a funeral tomorrow."

"But after that, you need to take some time off," the doctor said. "You need time for yourself, time to mend. Your blood sugar is out of whack, your weight is low, and I suspect you've been running on adrenaline for a long time."

"I'll make sure he takes it easy," I said. "I plan to stay in town for a while. I'll see to it he gets rest." I was sitting on the edge of Jake's bed, my hand on his. Jake rested back on the pillows, the bed elevated so he was more upright than reclined. His fingers squeezed mine when I said that. I saw Nick's surprised look at this announcement, but I didn't elaborate. As far as I was concerned, I'd stay while Jake needed me. I wasn't going to lose him, too.

Now we were just waiting for the doctors to sign Jake's discharge papers, and we'd take him home. Karl was already there. He went ahead to feed the cats and get things ready for Jake. He would stay with Jake tonight, and Sally would stay tomorrow night. I'd take over after that for a few days. "At least I have an open-ended ticket. I'd like to stay through the week. I know there's a bunch of paperwork and stuff he needs to work on because of Wil's death. Maybe I can help him."

"He'd appreciate that," Nick said. "I think we all would. It's hard when family lives far away. I'm glad I moved back here so I could be close to Mom. It always bothered me when I lived away because it was hard to stay in touch."

"I suppose I'm at that point with Jake." I rested my head in my hand, staring down at the plastic tabletop. "I'm the daughter who needs to think about taking care of Dad. It's weird. I don't think of him as elderly but he's getting there, isn't he?"

"It's not just the stress of Wil's death. He and Wil were worried about the inheritance and how it would affect you. He said they've been aware of pressure since summer. I know Wil was worried before that. They'd do anything to keep you from having to relive what happened."

"I wish I had known that. It doesn't matter that much to me. It's all in the past. It can't hurt me now."

Nick reached across the table and took my hand in his. "I don't think you understand how tough it could be. The Bose family will stop at nothing to discredit you. They want that inheritance. They'll do anything to get it."

"What about the old man?" I asked. "Doesn't he have any control over what they're doing?"

Nick leaned back, his hand slipping off mine. "I'm not sure. I've never met him. He's been a recluse for years. His lawyers handle all of his business affairs. He hasn't been seen extensively in public for some time."

"What do you think? Do you think he's right to do what he's doing? To disinherit his stepchildren in favor of a child he's never known?"

Nick frowned, staring at the table while he considered what to say. "It's his money to do with as he pleases," he finally said. "Let's face it, if he gives away his first wife's estate, it still leaves plenty of money for his second family."

"That's how you and I see it," I pointed out. "We'd think a few thousand dollars would be exciting. We're not thinking in the billionaire category."

"I suppose Richard Bose has to think that way. If

you want to be president, you need money behind you. And you need powerful friends. He has both, but it wouldn't hurt to have more of each. A billion dollars will buy you a lot of friends."

The buzzer gadget on the table between us thumped, blinking red. "Looks like we're being paged." I grabbed it and stood.

"That was faster than I thought it would be. Usually it takes forever to get released." Nick went with me to the door and out into the hall.

"Maybe because it's so late at night? Jake was so anxious to leave, they were probably happy to have him gone." We took a left at the next hallway and soon were at the emergency wing.

Jake was at the doorway to his tiny cubicle sitting in a wheelchair, a male orderly at the handles. "I got my rolling papers," he said, flourishing a sheaf of computer printouts.

I took them from him and looked around for the nurse on duty. "You guys go out to the car. I'll be along in a minute." I spied the woman I was looking for and made a sprint in her direction before she could vanish into a room.

I had a quick consult with her while reviewing the paperwork, then I was outside, dashing through the rain to the car. I slid into the back seat. "I just wanted to make sure I understood the directions," I said, dropping the pages onto the seat next to me.

"Take a pill when I get home, take one in the morning, and call my doctor on Monday." Jake waved a hand. "Sleep and rest. Like I'll have time to do any of that."

"You will have time because I'll be there to make

sure you do it." I tapped him on the shoulder for emphasis.

In a few minutes we were turning into the drive. Karl had the lights on at the house. I helped Jake inside while Nick parked the car in the garage. "The doctor said a brandy would be okay," Karl said, leading Jake to the recliner in the family room. "It won't interfere with the drugs they want him to take."

"Interfere, hell," Jake grumbled. "A touch of brandy never hurts."

I went to the linen closet near the downstairs bedroom and pulled out the worn cotton blanket from the bottom shelf. I tossed it into the dryer in the laundry room and rejoined Karl and Jake. "I'm warming up the hospital blanket," I said, leaning over Jake to kiss his cheek. "You wrap that around you before you go to bed."

"That blanket came home with you. I'm glad we kept it all these years." He rested his head against my arm briefly, then smiled at me.

"It's the Owie Blankie. That's what Wil always called it. Whenever you had an owie, all it took was a warmed-up blanket, a cookie, and a Band-Aid to make it better." I blinked back tears at the memory.

"She was right, too. It's good to have you here, Punzi. I've missed you."

I touched his thick white hair. "I've missed you, too." I meant it. It was so good to be around family again, around people who knew me and all about my odd life. I was home.

"You folks get some rest now," Jake said. "We don't have to be at the funeral place until eleven, so you sleep in. Stop on over here if you want to before the service or just meet us there."

I glanced at Nick. He was bent over the fire, poking at it. When he saw my look, he shook his head. "We'll meet you there. You make sure to get your rest tonight, too."

Karl settled into the other recliner, a glass of amber liquid in his hand. "We'll just shoot the breeze for a bit, then I'll tuck him in for the night. Sally said they'd come over tomorrow and make breakfast. You sure you don't want to have some of her pancakes?" He smiled wryly.

I laughed. Sally's pancakes could be used in place of hockey pucks. "I'll pass, thank you. We'll see you tomorrow." I squeezed Karl's shoulder, then Nick and I left, dashing through the rain to his car. He'd moved it, so it was just a few short steps to jump in.

"Thanks for all the help," I said as we drove through the darkness.

He didn't answer for a minute or two, then he said, "I owe Jake and Wil more than you know. They helped me through a really rough time when I was younger. I'm glad to help however I can."

"Was it because of the trial? Because of me?"

"It wasn't because of you. I mean, yes, it was, but it was bound to happen sooner or later. I was a new guy on the force. I had to learn the rules of the game. Wil and Jake helped me understand that."

I wanted to know more, but I could tell he didn't want to share. I stared out the window. The town was quiet, even the traffic lights now switched to simply blinking red. The entire area had the look of a hushed painting, like an advertisement for a small-town Christmas movie or TV show.

We arrived at the hotel and used our keycards to get into the lobby, which was locked up for the night. As we rode upstairs in the elevator, I felt curiously empty or hollowed out. Stress, probably, and the fear of losing Jake on top of losing Wil. And Bobby, I realized. Seeing him again. But it wasn't like seeing him. The man who confronted me was a stranger, not the teasing, laughing youth I remembered.

And yet Nick was like I remembered. Oh, yes, he was older. That smooth baby-soft complexion was gone. He was heavier, not the thin and slender boy-man who picked me up and carried me so gently to the squad car. But his sincerity and his willingness to help remained the same. I still saw compassion when I looked into his multi-colored gaze.

We got to the suite and Nick opened the door. I went immediately to the bar across the room and opened the fridge. "I need a glass of wine or maybe a shot of bourbon."

"I wouldn't mind sharing that with you."

The warmth in his voice made me shiver. There was an unmistakable huskiness in his tone. I was poised over a precipice, facing a choice waiting to happen. Be with him or not? Perhaps it was my exhaustion or my runaway emotions that made me say, "I think I'll just grab something and take it to bed. There must be a stupid movie on TV that'll put me to sleep." I didn't look at him to gauge his reaction. I just pulled open the mini-fridge and stared inside.

"That sounds like a good plan," he said, his voice neutral. I thanked God I didn't hear any disappointment there. I didn't need that guilt on top of everything else I was feeling. "You had a busy day today, and you'll have a busy one tomorrow, too."

I stared blindly into the small unit, finally focusing

on the miniature bottles of wine. I grabbed two white ones and turned. Nick was walking across the living space heading for his bedroom door. "Good night," I said.

He glanced over his shoulder. "Good night, Jessa. I hope you sleep well."

"Thank you. For everything."

He smiled faintly. "I'm happy to help." He disappeared into his room before I could even blink.

I took the two bottles of wine with me into my bedroom, draining one while I got out of my clothes, and pulled on my sleep T-shirt. I took my hair out of its confinement and shook it loose, brushing it out over my shoulders. I leaned forward to stare at myself in the mirror. My hair was beautiful, a mix of silver and white with some faint traces of the pale gold I had in my youth. The texture was still the same, too, soft and pliable. Bobby always said it was like liquid in his hands, so soft.

Bobby. I washed my face, the splash of water like a wake-up call on my brain. Why was he at Wil's visitation? I didn't buy his story of being with someone who wanted to pay their respects. Where was he living now? I couldn't remember what I'd been told, just that he moved away. Didn't he? Or was he still in town? The last few days were like a blur with all bits and pieces of conversation getting mixed up with each other. Who said what and when? I couldn't remember.

I smeared on some face cream, then took the second bottle of wine with me to the bedroom. I climbed into the bed and stared at the blank TV screen. Jake was worried about what would happen if I did submit to the test and was proven to be Miller's daughter. I could easily imagine him and Wil talking about it, working through all the things that might happen.

They had hidden me from the spotlight when I was rescued. It was years later that I found out just how much they shielded me from reporters, television producers, psychologists, and psychiatrists. Everyone wanted to know my story, everyone wanted to know my reaction to the *real* world. Wil and Jake allowed one psychiatrist and one psychologist to work with me. Those doctors helped Wil and Jake acclimate me to society. My story was not sold to any networks, nor was it documented in any textbooks except in general terms. Anything that might identify me was erased.

I thought back to all the comments I heard today about Wil. I had such difficulty trusting any man after what happened with Bobby. She and I had long conversations about sex and love and relationships. I had been so trusting and so naïve because I had no basis for comparison. I had no standard by which to judge what Bobby told me. "Unfortunately, you learn through experience," she told me once. "You can usually trust your heart, but just make sure you listen to your head, too."

I lay in bed, staring at the ceiling. I did trust Nick. He had traveled halfway across the country just to help me, all at Wil's behest. Wil. I wallowed in memories for a moment, tears rolling down my face. She was one of those women who was so memorable, so alive and full of energy. I had never met anyone like her. But I'd met very few people before meeting her, so maybe that's why I tried to model myself after her. Wil was fearless, going after what she wanted with a single-minded determination. I wasn't quite as focused, but I was persistent.

What would Wil do in my circumstance? I knew immediately. She'd take a chance. "A chance not taken is an opportunity missed," she used to say. "Even if it turns out wrong, you're on a new path that may lead to great things."

I threw the covers off. Before I could think of a reason to stop myself, I drained the second bottle of wine then stalked out of my bedroom. I crossed the living room, thankful that the curtains had been left open so I could see where I was going. I got to the door to Nick's bedroom, knocked once, then opened it.

He was in bed, lying on his back. The light was on in his bathroom but the door was mostly closed so the room was almost totally dark. "What's wrong?" He pushed back his covers and stood. He was bare-chested and naked except for boxer shorts.

"Look," I said. "I'm at the half-time of my life. If you don't want me, just say so." I stared defiantly at him, hands on my hips, my Hello Kitty T-shirt sagging off my shoulders.

"What?"

"You heard me." I stayed still while he moved toward me, my eyes widening at the sight of the expanse of male chest nearing me. "I think there's something between us, but I wasn't sure. Well, if there is, then let's, you know, let's explore it. And if there isn't, then just tell me." I was babbling, but it was probably the effect of two glasses of wine talking.

Nick looked down at me then smiled. The warmth of his odd-colored eyes reached all the way through my body, making me shiver with anticipation. "Come here, woman." He put his hands on my shoulders and pulled me to him.

"What?"

"You heard me. Come here." He scooped me up in his arms and lowered his face, his beard scraping against my cheek.

I wrapped my arms around his neck. "Come here?"

He moved me to the bed and came down, his body covering mine. "I hope so," he whispered.

I did.

****

I woke sometime during the night and stirred, touching the side of the bed where I thought Nick lay. It was empty. I sat up and peered around the darkened room.

"Go back to sleep," he said from somewhere on my left.

I reached out my hand. "Where are you?"

"Just had to use the bathroom. I'll be back in a second."

I fell asleep before my head reached the pillow.

When I woke again, faint sunlight shone behind the curtains on my right. I sat up, pulling the covers with me. The room was empty. I had the feeling the entire suite was empty. It had that echoing sense about it.

I pulled on my T-shirt and went to the bathroom door. "Nick?"

No answer. I went into the living room area. There was no sign of Nick anywhere, but a note was on the table near the window. *I ordered breakfast for 9:00. Be back soon.*

I glanced at the clock. It was eight, so I had plenty of time to get showered and dressed. I wandered into my bathroom and surveyed myself in the mirror. My cheeks were flushed, my hair was a mess, and I ached in places that hadn't ached in recent memory. I smiled. It felt good. I peeled off my T-shirt and got into the shower, luxuriating in the hot spray. I had just finished soaping when there was a knock on the bathroom door.

"Mind if I join you?" Nick called.

"I think there's room," I replied. A few seconds later, he ducked into the shower enclosure, his arms going around me.

"You're all slippery," he said, nuzzling against my neck.

"I guess that means you'll have to save me from falling."

He did just that, by lifting me and moving me against the shower wall. It had been a long time since I'd been so athletic, but we managed without any falls.

We were still in our hotel bathrobes when room service arrived with breakfast. There was a large bouquet of flowers on the trolley. "Who are those from?" I asked, sliding onto the chair nearest the window.

"I thought a spot of color would be nice," Nick said. "I got them this morning." He stood near the door. When the waiter left, he locked it, then joined me.

"Are you worried about something?" I asked, nodding at the door.

"No, not really. I doubt if anyone would attempt something in a public place like this. I just want to make sure we have privacy." He smiled at me across the table, looking boyish and young with his hair disarrayed and his beard freshly trimmed.

I surveyed the small feast in front of me. Muffins, bacon, scrambled eggs, and hash browns, all under serving cloches and waiting to be dished out. "How did you know what I like for breakfast?" I asked, helping myself to the eggs.

"I took a wild guess. And I asked Jake if there was anything you hated, so I could avoid it." Nick filled his plate then held up his glass of orange juice. "Here's to our great night together."

I clicked my glass against his. "I enjoyed it."

"I did, too. It's been a long time since I had so much fun." He took a bite of muffin. "What did you mean last night when you said you were at the half-time of life?"

"Well, if life's a football game, this is half-time." I held up my hands. "Almost the third quarter."

"If life is a football game, then I feel like I just won the Super Bowl."

I waggled my fork at him. "Quit it. You'll inflate my ego."

"I mean it, Jessa. I've had a great time with you, even when we weren't in bed together. I wish it could last."

"I'll be here for a few more days," I said.

"Not enough time."

"We'll see how things shape up. I may be coming out to visit more often now that I know Jake needs my help."

"It's not just Jake who needs you," he said softly.

I considered how to answer that, but I was saved by a text from Karl. I peered at the phone. "Jake just woke up. Karl said he slept all night. Sally is coming over soon."

"I hope he doesn't eat any of her cooking. It'll offset any progress he's made. We should probably get to the funeral home by eleven-thirty. It's going to be a simple service. If anyone wants to speak, they can."

"I'd like to, I think. Wil meant a lot to me." I

considered what to say and just like that, we were off the tricky topic of a possible relationship and back to thinking about the upcoming day. I ran some thoughts by Nick and he suggested some other ideas. Soon it was almost ten o'clock. "I need to get ready," I said. "Someone interrupted my shower."

"Guilty as charged." Nick pushed back from the table and came around it to take me in his arms when I stood. "I meant what I said, Jessa. I had a great time." He brushed a kiss against my lips.

I hugged him, then moved away. "I did, too. And I meant what I said. I think I'll be spending more time here in town. I didn't realize that Jake...I didn't think that he needed me, but I think he does."

"I know he does. What about your store?"

I shrugged. "I'll consider that. Later. Right now, I have to get ready." I went to my bedroom, pausing by the bouquet of flowers to touch one rose. "Thank you for the color."

"It can be awfully gray here in the wintertime. Maybe you need to talk Jake into taking some trips somewhere warm and sunny after Christmas. I'd be happy to join you."

"Good idea." I went into my bedroom, glancing at the window when I passed. Nick was right. This was a gray and wet place in winter. At least in Iowa we got snow to cover up the ugly brown grass and the dead leaves. A trip to Hawaii or somewhere like that might be just what the doctor ordered for Jake.

I took another quick shower, then dressed in my second funeral outfit, the dark pants and dark blouse with embroidered roses on the collar. I wore a dark red sweater vest that Wil gave me for Christmas the year before. I touched the Wonder Woman pin she also gave me and which I kept on the vest. "You remind me of Wonder Woman," she'd said. "Raised away from the world and thrown into it with so little warning."

"I wish I had a golden lasso," I had replied. "That would save a lot of headaches, wouldn't it?"

She'd laughed and hugged me. "Trust your instincts and you can't go wrong."

"Thank you, Wil." I brushed away a tear and applied some makeup, then tackled my hair, which was still damp. I bent over and brushed it up into a loose ponytail. I created a braid and experimented with it, finally rolling it into a circle that I pinned in place. A few wisps of hair were left around my face. I was ready to meet the day.

I grabbed my small handbag, peeking inside to make sure I had my key card. I spied Janice's little good luck charm and pulled it out to make the bell ring. Maybe there was something to it, I thought. It was good luck that brought Nick back into my life. I examined the Japanese character on the cat's tummy. It did look like a button of some kind. I made sure to tuck it away in a spot where I wouldn't inadvertently set off the alarm.

The living room was empty when I entered. I went to the window. It was foggy again but not as heavy as the previous day. Maybe we'd even see some sun today. My phone thumped against my hip where it rested in the bag. I pulled it out and recognized the number. "This is Jessa."

"Hi, this is Wanda Bose. Do you know your schedule yet? I'd like to meet today."

"I don't know for sure. I think I'll have some free time this afternoon."

"Great. I can make that work. Where would you like

to meet? You're staying at the Arms, aren't you? We could meet at the restaurant if you'd like. Maybe for a drink this afternoon?"

"I'm not sure," I repeated. "Why don't I call you this afternoon?" Nick's bedroom door opened and he came out, dressed again in his dark suit pants and jacket.

"Sure, that works. Like I said, we have the fundraiser tonight. It's at our stepfather's house. My mother is hosting it. Hey, maybe you should come out and join us."

"I don't have a hundred dollars sitting around to donate to your cause." I rolled my eyes, pulling the phone away slightly. "Wanda Bose," I said softly when Nick joined me.

He shook his head. "You really shouldn't meet with her."

"I'll call you later," I said to the phone, then I ended the call. "She thought I might want to attend a fundraiser tonight for her brother."

"Really?"

"I politely declined." I reached up to straighten Nick's necktie. "You look very handsome all dressed up."

"Thank you. I like your pin." He touched the enameled W. "Wonder Woman is one of my favorite superheroes."

"Like I told Wil, I wish I had a golden lasso. Then I could always tell if someone was lying or not."

Nick stepped back. "Sometimes a small lie is a good thing."

"Maybe," I said. "If it's a small lie about a small thing." He turned away. I thought I saw him wince or maybe frown. "Is that a problem?"

"No, of course not." He picked up the vase of flowers. "I thought we'd take these with us to the funeral home. Something colorful and pretty for Wil."

"That's a great idea." I picked up my coat from the couch where I'd tossed it the night before. "I suppose we should get over there and help Jake deal with the relatives."

"At least it's a small crowd today." Nick held the door for me and we went to the elevator. While we rode downstairs, he said, "There's something I need to discuss with you after the service."

"Why not discuss it now?"

He stared at the elevator doors. I could tell from the tense line of his shoulders what his answer would be. "I'd rather wait. I think we need to focus on Jake and Wil right now and not on anything that might be distracting."

I took his hand. "You've been distracting me all morning."

He didn't smile like I expected him to. Instead he just squeezed my fingers and said, "I think Jake needs our support. He's been a big help to me in the past, and I want to help him now." Nick glanced down at me and smiled, but it was a fake smile, or maybe a sad one. I couldn't tell. "Let's just get through today."

For some reason I had the idea that he wasn't talking about the funeral service. I nodded. "Sure. Let's get through it."

Whatever *it* was.

Chapter 10

I held the vase of flowers while we drove to the funeral home. Their fragrance was very faint but persistent. It was like the feeling I had about what Nick said. I knew he was going to tell me something that I'd find uncomfortable or, worse, that would change my opinion of him.

I didn't want that. I wanted to hold on to the happy thought that I might have something in the future with him. I knew that distance would give us challenges. I was okay with that. I was okay with the chance that any relationship wouldn't survive that. I didn't want our chance to be nipped in the bud before we had the opportunity.

I fingered the flowers, rearranging them in the vase. I had no control over what he was going to tell me. Nick was right. I had to support Jake today, and whatever happened after this service, well, I'd handle it. Lord knows I had enough experience handling unpleasant things.

After all, I wasn't in love with Nick. I wasn't sure what I felt, but this wasn't undying love. This was a man who knew my past, so it was easy with him. I could relax around him. That in itself was unusual. I didn't realize it until it happened, but I had been hiding my past life from the men I'd known. I didn't have to hide anything with Nick. He knew it all.

I looked out my window, and as I did, the sun broke through the clouds. I leaned back, smiling. "It's nice to see sunshine. It's been cloudy since I arrived."

"Enjoy it while it lasts. We don't often get these breaks."

I touched his hand. "I will enjoy it while it lasts."

He glanced at me. "So will I."

"It doesn't matter what you say, Nick. Please don't worry about it."

He didn't answer but only nodded. We didn't speak again until we got to the funeral home. Nick parked the car, and we went into the building. Like yesterday, someone was there to greet us, this time showing us to a smaller, more private space on the right side of the building. It held just a dozen or so chairs, with a podium at the far end of the room. Wil's pictures were on a table at the side.

We hung up our coats and joined Jake and the others who were standing at the table. When Jake saw us, he walked through the chairs. He looked rested, with some color in his cheeks and none of the haggard grief I saw yesterday. "Did you sleep okay last night?" I asked.

"Those pills and the brandy did the trick. Combined with the Owie Blanket, I passed out like a light." He released me and looked at Nick. "How about you two?"

"Just fine." I held up the vase. "We brought these for the table."

"Pretty. Thank you." Jake stepped aside, he and Nick moving to the entryway.

I joined Karl at the table with the photographs. "How did he do last night?" I whispered.

"Fine. We talked for a time. Cried a bit. He's doing better today. I think having you here is a big help. I hope you can stay for a few days." Karl straightened one of the photos, a picture of me and Wil at the house with the barn cats romping around our feet.

"I plan to," I promised. "And I'm going to see if I can come back in a few weeks for Christmas and maybe stay for a week or two." The words came out unplanned, but I was glad I said it. "I can take more time off next year, too. I have an assistant at the store who's been itching to try her hand at managing."

"You're lucky to have somebody like that you can count on."

"I know. She'll do a great job, too." I moved around the table, examining the pictures, some of which I'd never seen. "Do you know if they have any leads on who might have killed her? I know these things take time, but Wil was a judge. Wouldn't she get priority?"

Karl put his arm around my shoulders and squeezed me. "Knowing who did it won't make it any easier."

"No, but it might make me feel better to know somebody will pay for what they did."

"She was well respected in town. The police are doing the best they can." He released me. "Looks like we're getting started."

Jake came toward me. "We're going to have her eulogy read. Then if anybody wants to speak, they can."

I nodded. "I will." I had no idea what I'd say, but I had to say something. I looked around for Nick, but he wasn't in sight.

"He's checking with the guy he has on duty," Jake said.

"Guy on duty?"

"I guess he's doing it right if you don't even notice him." Jake went to a seat in front and I followed him.

"Do you really think there's a danger to me?"

"After what happened with Wil, I'm not taking any chances." Jake sat, Sally sliding into the seat next to him.

I was so surprised, I didn't move. Good Lord, is that how he was thinking? Why didn't I consider that? I sank down into a chair in the row behind Jake, my mind whirling. He'd lost the woman he loved, and he was concerned that the woman he considered a daughter was in danger. No wonder the poor man almost had a heart attack.

I leaned back in the chair. What could I do to make this all go away? If I gave them a hair sample, at least everything would be out in the open. There would be none of this cat and mouse game. Maybe that's what I should do. That might end if once and for all.

But what if it proved that I was the lost daughter? I did not want to inherit a fortune and a fight with a bunch of strangers. I'd give the money away. That was the simplest solution. I'd set up some kind of charitable trust or something, give a bunch of money to the Bose family to shut them up, and give the rest away.

Although I hated the thought of giving any money to Richard Bose. He was the kind of politician I hated, a self-righteous so-called patriot who longed to return America to its bigoted and misogynistic past. Maybe there was some way I could tie it up so no money could be used for any political support.

Nick sat beside me. "You're deep in thought," he murmured.

I blew out a sigh. "This whole heiress business has me wondering what to do."

"Maybe you should meet Miller. Hear what he has to say."

I started to dismiss the idea, then stopped. Why was I so opposed to hearing what the old man wanted to say to me? What was I afraid of? Because I *was* afraid, afraid that he might say something that would disturb the way I had framed my entire past. I had been the victim, discarded and bereft. But what if he had searched for me? What if it had been a desperate move on his part? Because of me, laws were changed. Those laws had helped dozens of children who might have otherwise ended up like I did, handed off to strangers. Or worse, left to die.

I turned my attention to the funeral director, who was approaching the podium. I needed to find some time to just sit down, think it through, and decide what to do. Watching Jake's face as the eulogy was read told me what was important. I needed to find a solution that would provide him with some peace of mind. I would handle whatever consequences came about because of my decision.

I listened to the man read Wil's obituary, then the eulogy that had been written by a colleague. She had led an interesting life, a life of service and a life devoted to helping other people. I was the recipient of that help. I owed it to her to do something similar with my life, the life that she helped mold.

When the director asked if anyone would like to speak, I knew exactly what I wanted to say. I stood and went to the front of the room, turning to face the small group of family and the few of Wil's co-workers who attended.

"Most of you know me, but for those who don't, I'm the girl in the tower," I said, my eyes scanning the people watching me. "Wil was appointed my guardian when I was found at age seventeen, after being isolated from the world for my entire life. I knew a world existed outside the house where I was kept, but I was not allowed to interact with it. I had no idea that it was even possible for me to live anywhere but where I did."

I held onto the podium, searching for the right words to encompass what Wil had done for me. "It's hard to explain to someone who wasn't raised the way I was, but Wil understood. She listened to what I told her. She managed to make me understand that I had a whole world ahead of me if I wanted it. She knew that my past was my reality, and now I was facing an entirely new reality. Wil helped me navigate that new reality. She showed me how to form new values and new rules for living without imposing her own assumptions on me."

I smiled at Jake, who watched me with rapt attention. "When I met Jake, I finally understood what the term 'father' meant. He welcomed me into their home and never once begrudged my intrusion into their lives." Movement in the middle of the room caught my eye. Nick stood, pulling a phone out of his pocket, his gaze intent on the display. I forced my attention back to what I was saying while he hurried from the room. "Jake and Wil showed me love and humor and a sense of social structure that I didn't know existed. They were the best role models anyone could ever hope for. I owe everything to them."

I drew in a deep breath, fighting back tears. "I'd call Wil whenever I had a question or whenever I wasn't sure how to go forward. We'd chat for a bit then she'd say something like 'Well, Punzi, you know it's always better to jump right in because trying to enter the pool one inch at a time is a bigger shock.' She was referring to the first time I saw a swimming pool." I smiled at Jake. "Remember?" He nodded. "We went to a friend's house and I stood there, not sure what to do. I didn't know how to swim. I had no concept of the idea of simply swimming for enjoyment. I didn't really understand leisure time or hobbies or anything like that. Wil and I stood there looking at the water, and she pushed me in. It was the shallow end, so all I did was go under for a second then I came bouncing back up. She jumped in and hugged me. I was so shocked I wasn't sure what to do. But she showed me how to float, then eventually I got swimming lessons. Soon I knew just what she meant. Jump right in and get it over with. She was that way about everything, fearless and strong. She was the best teacher I could ever have had. I'll miss her very much."

I made my way back to my chair, tears making the short walk difficult. I wiped at my eyes with my hankie, noticing for the first time that Karl was gone, too. I twisted in my seat to look around the room but neither Karl nor Nick was in sight. I turned my attention to one of Wil's co-workers who got up to speak about her work in the court system. A few minutes later, Karl came back into the room, taking a seat next to Sally, but Nick didn't return.

Two other people got up to talk, then Jake made his way to the front of the room. "I want to thank all of you who came out today to support me and to help me remember Wil. Everything you said is a comfort to me today. Remembering it will be a comfort to me in the future. I'll be going out in the springtime with family members to scatter her ashes. It's what she wanted, and it's fitting, I think. She was always a free spirit." He paused and swallowed convulsively then he smiled wanly. "We're going to have a bit of lunch now, so if you'd like to stay and join us, please do."

Jake left the podium and came to me. "You can stay for a sandwich, can't you, Punzi?"

"Of course." I sprang to my feet and looped my arm through his. "It was a nice service," I said while we walked out of the room, following the funeral director.

"It was what she wanted. All the public stuff was yesterday. Today was for close friends and family. Thank you for speaking. She always worried if she was setting a good example for you because she knew you really didn't have any role models."

We went into a small room where a simple buffet was laid out. Jake turned to talk to one of Wil's co-workers. I made my way to the food, putting bread, cold meat, and potato salad on a plate. I spied Karl and made a beeline for him. "Where did Nick go?" I asked. "You guys left the room at about the same time."

"He asked me to tell you. He got a call about his mother. There was a problem at the nursing home where she lives. She fell down or something. So he had to leave. But he has a friend of his doing guard duty out in the lobby. He'll drive you wherever you need to go and stick with you until Nick can get back."

"I hope everything's okay." I considered calling Nick, but decided he didn't need any distractions. "I know Nick's close to his mother."

"He said he'd give you a call later and update you." Karl moved away to talk to someone, and I took my plate to a small table. Several of Wil's co-workers joined me with their plates.

"I remember when your case came up," one of the older men said. "We discussed it in the office, about how to handle it. I think upper management wanted the social services office to handle your care, but Wil convinced them that it made more sense to make her your guardian. You had so little understanding about social systems, she was afraid you'd get lost in all the red tape. Plus you were in the hospital, weren't you? At least at first? She spent a lot of time with you. A social worker wouldn't have been able to give you the kind of attention she did."

"I was lucky," I said. "I never really thought about how I got assigned to her and Jake. I think you're right. If I'd been thrown into the social services system, Lord knows where I might have ended up."

"Now there's this whole inheritance thing, too," one of the women chimed in. "We've heard that Miller is looking for his daughter."

I almost dropped my sandwich. "Really? I didn't realize it was public knowledge."

"Oh, not really public knowledge," she assured me. "But word gets around different social circles. Stephanie Bose has made no secret of the fact she thinks her husband is crazy. I know Wil was worried about the publicity and how it might affect you."

"It's amazing what they can do now with scientific testing," the older man said. "Of course, in order to do a full forensic workup, they'd need a hair with the follicle intact. But any strand of hair that's cut will be enough to prove or disprove matrilineal descent. And apparently that's all Miller is concerned with." He eyed my upswept braid speculatively.

"Jessa has some decisions to make." Jake sat down next to me, a pile of potato chips on his plate.

"You need more than that," I chided.

"And I'll get more later." He looked around the

table. "Thank you all for coming. Work was a big part of Wil's life. I'm glad you were able to take the time to be here."

They murmured condolences. Then the woman said, "I think they were going to review all of the security tapes to try to identify the killer."

"It was probably somebody hired," the man said. "I'm sure there are goons for hire if you know where to look for them."

Goons for hire? I smiled at the image while they chatted about some of the cases Wil and Jake had worked on.

"Speaking of goons, there's a rather large man in the foyer," one of the co-workers said. "Loitering about."

"That must the guard Nick assigned to help." Jake stood, looking down at me. "Karl said Nick was called away."

I nodded. "I'll talk to him later to make sure things are okay."

"Good. I think I'll mingle a bit."

"Take it easy, Jake. Don't wear yourself out."

He put a hand on my shoulder. "This is good for me," he said softly. "I like talking about her with her friends. I'll be careful." He moved to the next table, hand outstretched to one of the people there.

"Is he okay? Problems?" the older man asked.

"The doctors just want him to relax a bit. Once all this is done, I hope he will. I think I'll mingle, too." I took my plate to the small table set aside for used dinnerware then looked around the room. Before I could decide on a new spot, my phone thumped in the small purse slung over my shoulder.

I left the room, pulling out the phone to check to see

if it was Nick calling. I stood in the foyer, frowning at the display. I recognized the number. "Hello, Miss Bose," I said, walking away from the room to go to the front door and peer outside.

"I know you said you weren't sure about your schedule, but I wanted to let you know that my stepfather is anxious to talk to you. I told him I've been in touch with you. He wondered if you could meet him."

I almost hung up on her. Didn't she listen? I was in town for a funeral. Now she wanted to add more stress on top of stress? No, she didn't listen or if she did, she didn't care. "I'm not sure that would be wise," I said, pacing in front of the wide front doors to watch the sunlight bouncing off car hoods. "I don't want to get his hopes up if it turns out I'm not his daughter."

I turned and when I did, I spied the *goon* standing near the far door. He wore a nicely tailored suit that almost disguised his bulky shoulders and muscular frame. His head was shaved. His eyes were dark and almost hidden under thick dark eyebrows.

When he saw my attention, he nodded once and turned his gaze back to the room where Jake and the others were gathered. "I'm sure he'd appreciate it," Bose said. "Just for a few minutes."

I glanced at the phone to check the time. It was almost two o'clock. I wanted to take a nap before going back to Jake's house in the evening. "Why don't you meet me at my hotel? We can discuss it there. I'm in Suite Three on the third floor. I'll let the front desk know you're coming." Maybe if I met with her, she'd leave me alone.

"Perfect. What time?"

"Half an hour?"

"I'll be there." She hung up so fast I know she was afraid I'd change my mind.

I went to the goon guard. "You're working with Nick, right?" Stupid question. Who else would it be? I didn't wait for his answer. "I need a ride to the hotel to meet with someone. Can you drive me?"

"Sure. That's what I'm here for." His voice was surprisingly not the deep rumbly sound I expected but more soft, almost whispery.

"Okay, good. I'll be ready in a minute." I hurried back to the buffet room and cornered Karl. "I'm heading back to the hotel with that guard Nick has on duty. I want to rest a bit before coming to the house tonight. I'll wait until I see if I hear from Nick, and we'll be over later on. Or else I'll come over and wait for him with you guys."

"That sounds good. I'll let Jake know, and I'll make sure he doesn't wear himself out."

"Thanks, Karl. For everything."

He just smiled and turned to greet another person who approached. I went out to the foyer to the coat rack. I got my coat, and the guard came forward and took it from me, holding it so I could slip it on.

"Thank you," I said, surprised by the gentlemanly gesture.

He led the way out of the building, holding the door for me then took my arm, steering me toward a large black sedan. "What's your name?" I asked.

"Ron. If you don't mind, I'd like you to sit in back."

I started to ask why but he didn't give me the chance. He just opened the door. I slid into the interior. He closed it then went around to the driver's side and got in. A few seconds later, we were underway.

There was something in the way Ron drove or acted

that told me he wouldn't welcome conversation. I sat back on the seat and tried to frame what I would say when I met Wanda Bose. She was my stepsister, a woman in a family I knew nothing about. From what Jake told me, August Miller had raised her and acted as a father to her.

Why was she so insistent on reaching out to me? What were her motives? If I were proven to be the daughter, her family would lose a substantial amount of money when her stepfather died. There was still a lot of money that remained, but perhaps to rich people, that didn't matter. I had money, but nothing like what they had. My settlement from the university had been invested for me. It provided me a nice little income in addition to what I made at the store.

The rich are different than you and I. Scott Fitzgerald was right. People in the billionaire world had completely different standards and values. Perhaps that's why Richard Bose bothered me so much. I hated posturing politicians, the ones who claimed they understood the working man all the while they were sipping champagne and golfing on the taxpayer's dime.

I wondered how much money it would take to buy off the Bose family. Of course, I didn't even know how much money we were talking about here. Jake had said billions, but that covered a wide range of dollars. I'd cross that bridge when I got to it. Right now I had to meet with this woman, get rid of her, then give myself some breathing room to make a decision about how to handle all of this mess. I also itched to call Nick, but I wasn't sure if I should. What if something had happened to his mother, and he was busy? But if something happened, then I wanted to help if I could.

These conundrums kept my thoughts busy until we pulled into the parking lot at the hotel. When I reached for the car door, I realized there was no handle. Ron came around the side and unlocked it with the key fob, opening the door for me. "Where are the handles? Why was it locked?" I asked. "I didn't see where to unlock it."

"Safety precaution," he said, walking beside me to the lobby.

We went inside, passed the check-in desk, and headed for the elevators. "I'm on the third floor," I said, rummaging in my bag for the keycard. "Oh, wait. I need to tell the desk I'll have a guest coming."

"I'll do it. Wait here." He vanished around the corner and came back a few seconds later. The elevator came and he stepped inside, then gestured me to join him. We rose to the upper floor. When I approached the door, he took the keycard from me and inserted it. "Wait here." He vanished inside before I could protest.

I peeked around the door to see him striding around the rooms, his hand poised over his waistband. Was he carrying a gun? I suppose if Nick did, this guard guy did, too. It was an unsettling thought.

He soon waved to me to come in. "Who are you expecting?"

"A woman," I said. "Wanda Bose. I'm not sure what she looks like."

"I know what she looks like. I've seen her picture. I'll wait in the foyer for her, and I'll stay out here so you have some privacy."

"Thank you. I'm not sure that's necessary."

"I'll wait out here." He left the suite before I could finish the sentence.

"What a rude man," I muttered. I hung my coat and

purse on the hook in the entryway, then went to the bedroom and reapplied some makeup before returning to the living area. I had just sat down to relax when a knock came on the door. It opened and a woman swept into the room.

Swept was the only word to use. She was tall with waist-length dark hair and the sort of slender build I'd only seen in runway models. Her clothing seemed composed of flowing layers of textiles, a loose sweater, an opened camel-hair coat flung back over her shoulders, a long scarf, and wide-leg pants tucked into knee-high boots with impossibly tall heels. It was all color coordinated in tones of brown, gold, and beige. It all screamed Money with a capital M. They were items of clothing that I saw in the pages of *Vanity Fair* or *Marie Claire,* the magazines sitting around the beauty shop where I had my hair cut.

"Hi, I'm Wanda Bose." She crossed the room in a few long strides and grabbed my hand, giving it a brisk shake. She wasn't a pretty woman, but she had the sort of face that was noticed mainly because of impeccable makeup and dark eyebrows over startling blue eyes. It was hard to guess her age. I knew she in her thirties, but she was the kind of woman who would probably appear to be the same age for decades. "You look like her."

"I beg your pardon?" I peered up at her. Between the boots and her own slender build, she was almost six feet tall.

"You look like her. The first wife." She moved past me to the windows. "I've never been in this hotel. It's nice. This used to be a rundown old hovel. I wasn't sure what they'd do with it, but it's very well done. I know the designer they brought in. She did the entryway in my apartment. I had a consultant from L.A. do the main living area, but the local woman was good. I'm glad they kept the view. It would be shame to lose that." Bose glanced over her shoulder at me. "It's quite expensive. I'm surprised you're staying here."

She said it with a naïve simplicity that told me she didn't realize how insulting her comment was. As the stepdaughter of a rich man, she'd probably been insulated from the real world all of her life. "Do you mean August Miller's first wife?" I asked politely.

She turned and sank into a chair, like a graceful gazelle folding up her legs and simply dropping onto the upholstered cushion. "Yes. Her name was Cindy. He has a picture of her in his study. You look like her. Your hair is the same. My mother's hair is blonde, too, but it's not white like yours. I always wondered if that's why he married her. Because she looked like his first wife."

Nothing like spilling the family secrets, I thought, taking a seat opposite her on the couch. "Weren't they in love?"

Bose shrugged, the action making her sweater and coat slide over her shoulders. "I don't know. I was just a kid when they got married. My father died after I was born. I think maybe Mother loved Stepdaddy, but I don't know if he ever really loved her. I always had the feeling he was sad. Maybe he got married hoping it would fill a void." She tilted her head to regard me, wide blue eyes apparently innocent and trusting.

"You're very forthcoming to be talking to a stranger like this."

"But you're not really a stranger, are you? Once it's proven you're my stepsister, we'll all be part of the same family."

"I don't know if we're at that point," I said slowly. "There's a lot of things I need to know about before I decide to do it."

"Look, I wanted to thank you for providing the hair sample. It will quiet my stepfather's mind to know if you are his daughter. He'll know that you've overcome what happened and have made a good life for yourself." She regarded me with a bright smile. "He's really been obsessing about it a lot lately."

"I don't understand. I didn't provide a sample yet. I'm still considering it."

"Nick Kingson dropped it off this morning. I like you. I think we can work this out and be friends. We don't have to be enemies."

"I'm sorry. What?"

"Kingson. He dropped off a sample this morning. My stepfather was so excited."

Nick took a sample of my hair to them? "What?"

"I said we don't have to be enemies. Not like Nick Kingson and Bobby. They hate each other. But we don't have to be that way. We can be stepsiblings and still get along."

"Bobby?" I could barely articulate the word.

"Sure. Bobby Reagan. He and Nick are stepbrothers. Didn't you know?"

Chapter 11

I was on my feet but I didn't remember standing. "That's not possible."

Wanda Bose peered up at me, frowning, her perfectly outlined lips pursed in a pout. "Sure it is. I know Bobby Reagan and I know Nick Kingson. Nick's mom married Bobby's dad. I think Bobby's kind of creepy, actually. He's an ogler. You know, one of those old guys who likes to leer at younger women. They're everywhere, aren't they?"

My mother remarried when I was twelve. I got a stepfather and a stepbrother in that deal.

"This is a small town, socially speaking," Wanda continued, unaware of my turmoil. "Everybody knows everybody else's business. They're older than me, of course, but Bobby runs around in the same circles I do."

My mom loved corny things It drove my stepfather crazy.

The Reagans moved out of Rampian after the trial.

The father died. I'm not sure who's left.

My stepfather died. I don't stay in touch with my stepbrother.

She loved those Christmas crackers with the corny jokes inside.

What do you call a broke Santa? Saint Nickle-less.

"Hello? Are you okay?" Wanda Bose stood in front of me, staring into my eyes. "You look like you've seen a ghost."

I had to talk to Nick. I had to find out why he lied to me. Wait a minute. He didn't lie to me. He just didn't tell me. A sin of omission?

"I think you should sit down." Wanda gestured to the chair behind me. I sat, barely noticing where I was. My mind couldn't encompass it all.

My attacker was Nick's stepbrother.

"I'm surprised you didn't know. Didn't Nick tell you? Of course, they aren't close." Wanda sprawled on the couch, her long legs stretched out and crossed. "Everybody knows it was Nick's testimony that sent him to prison."

Nick took a lot of heat for testifying at the trial.

You'd have as much in common with Richard Bose as Nick does with his stepbrother.

Good God. Jake knew. Wil had known. Why didn't they tell me?

"Nick had to leave town after the trial. His stepfather disowned him. I think his stepfather divorced his mother. Or there was something." Wanda shrugged again. "Like I said, this is all just old gossip. When Nick moved back here, I heard about it. Bobby Reagan belongs to the same country club I belong to. People talk. It's odd. I heard one time that his father was involved with the mob or some kind of illegal stuff. His father lost a bunch of money. I wouldn't be surprised. Bobby's kind of creepy, in an old guy way." Wanda examined one fingernail critically. "I don't remember what it was about."

I was having a hard time getting a breath. I needed to find Nick, to find Jake, to find the truth.

"Will you do it? Will you meet with him? Oh, yeah. That's right. I have a note to give to you." Wanda dug into her coat pocket and pulled out a crumpled piece of paper. "Here." She thrust it at me.

I unfolded it, my fingers cold and numb. The handwriting was tidy and angular, all aligned perfectly. Handwriting is a lost art, I thought randomly.

You don't know me, but I believe I'm your father. Although from what I've been told, Jake Brothers really holds that title, and I don't begrudge him that. I searched for you for years. It was just in the last few months that I got a clue that you might still be alive.

I'd like to see you and talk to you. I know you don't owe me anything. Perhaps you're thinking this is too little, too late. Maybe it is. But I'm an old man, and I'd like to see the child who was born to the woman I loved so much. Please. Let me talk to you.

August Miller

I folded the note. "What happened in the last few months?"

"Hmm?"

"He said he got a clue in the last few months that I was alive. That's why he initiated a search to find me."

Wanda gave another of those pouty frowns. "I'm not sure. I think Richard's people had something to do with that. They were doing background checks on everybody in the family. You know how politicians are. They want to know all the dirt there is to know, so they know it first and can make it look like it isn't dirt. Maybe they uncovered you. Are you going to see him?" She gestured to the note I held.

I stared down at the note. Nick had already given them a sample of my hair. Why did he do it? When did he do it? I pushed those thoughts aside, not sure what I felt. Meet the old man? Why not? Did it matter if I met the old man or not? "I suppose."

"Good." She beamed at me. "I told him I'd convince you. Come on. Let's go." She bounded to her feet and held out a hand.

"Now?" I peered up at her, so disoriented I wasn't even sure what day it was, much less what time of day.

"Sure. We have that thing tonight, that fundraiser for my brother. It starts at five. Some people will probably come early. You know, the people who want favors. It doesn't matter about them. But you can come over now for a few minutes at least. You're not really dressed for the fundraiser. It's all black tie and satin gowns. I know it would mean a lot to him." She bounced to the door. "Come on. I like him, you know. I mean, he's not my real father, but he's been good to me. I'd like to help him if I can."

I stared down at the note, then dropped it on the coffee table. I followed her, picking up my jacket and purse from the entryway hook. Ron the guard stood near the elevator. "I'm going with Miss Bose to her home," I told him.

"I'll drive," he said, tapping the elevator button.

"My car is here," Wanda said. "I can drive."

"I'll drive, then I'll bring you back here to pick up your car." He regarded her impassively when she pouted at him.

"Oh, okay. Whatever." She flounced ahead of him into the elevator car.

"I don't think that's necessary," I said. "I'm willing to talk with Mr. Miller, so I don't think there's any reason for you to be involved."

He tapped the lobby button. "I have my orders."

I started to argue, but Wanda said, "I can send over

one of Richard's people to pick up the car, so it's fine."

"Okay, if you're sure," I muttered, glaring at Ron's back.

He led the way out of the elevator and to the parking lot and the black sedan. Wanda and I were soon in the back seat. He drove out of the lot, heading west toward town. "We live out on East Port Road," Wanda said, leaning over the seat. "It's in the Castle Town subdivision."

Ron nodded and continued driving. "He's not very sociable," Wanda said softly.

I shrugged. "It wasn't my decision to have a driver."

Nick gave them a sample of my hair. Why? It would have been easy enough to do, I suppose. He had access to my hairbrush. Hell, last night he and I were tumbling around in bed together. I flushed, remembering when he pulled me on top of him, my hair brushing against his chest. He got up in the night. Did he cut off some of my hair then?

I touched my head, then mentally gave myself a slap. All it required was a few strands of hair. I wouldn't miss those and certainly couldn't tell if they were gone.

"He said that you didn't know anything about us until a few days ago," Wanda said.

We were in close quarters in the back seat, and I smelled her perfume. I never wore fragrances, so I had no idea what it was, but if it was like her purse, her boots, and her clothes, it was pricy. Despite her obvious Rich Bitch persona, I liked her. She appeared to be exactly what she seemed to be with no pretense at being anyone else. So many people presented a façade, but not her. This was her, pure and simple. I admired that in a person.

"Are you part of your brother's campaign staff?" I

asked. "Are you organizing the fundraiser tonight?"

"Oh, crap, no," she said with a laugh. "I've got nothing to do with that, and believe me, Richard is happy that I'm keeping my distance. No, I'm the ditzy younger sister who smiles at people, introduces him as my loving older bro, then I leave the stage." She tilted her head toward me. "I don't mind at all. I can't stand politics, and the farther I can stay away from it, the better."

"Are you worried that I might inherit money that your family deserves?"

She shrugged. "Mom said she'd sue you in court if you try, so it's probably not going to be much of an impact on me. Besides, it's Stepdaddy's money, not mine. He can do what he wants. He's promised me an allowance no matter what."

"What do you mean, 'no matter what'?" We were passing the road to Jake and Wil's house. I stared outside, wondering if the funeral party was heading home yet. My phone thumped against my side. I fumbled it out and stared at the display.

Nick.

"Do you need to take that call?" Wanda asked. "That's okay. I won't listen."

"No." I put the phone away. How could I talk to him knowing what I knew? But I wanted to talk to him, to find out about his mother. But how could I? "What were you saying?" I asked, my brain struggling to process too much information.

"I said I was going to be taken care of whether he found you or not. Stepdaddy and I always got along fine. It's Richard he can't stand." She wrinkled her nose. "Richard is a stuck-up prig. He and Mom are two of a kind. I guess I take after my dad, but I wouldn't know because he died so long ago. Anyway, Stepdaddy's already set up a trust fund for me, and I get an allowance every month. He bought me a condo downtown. If I don't get too extravagant, I'll be fine." She smiled brightly at me. "I told you. He's taking care of me, so it doesn't matter what you do. No, it's Mom and Richard who care. It's a lot of money." We had reached the highway and Ron made a turn, merging with the heavier traffic. "We're three or four exits ahead," Wanda said, leaning forward to talk to him.

He nodded and kept driving.

"I'm surprised you feel that way," I said. "It's a lot of money."

"After the first million or so, it doesn't really matter. I mean, a person can only have so many homes or clothes or jewelry, right?"

I nodded dumbly, stunned by her offhand comment.

"Let's face it, I'm much better off than most people. If my lifestyle doesn't suffer because of you, I really don't care. And Stepdaddy has made sure it won't."

"But your mother feels differently?" I managed to croak.

Wanda sighed, a big gesture that made her coat and sweater bounce. "My mother keeps score. She's one of those people who knows exactly what somebody paid for a car or a house or how much money they bring home or what clubs they belong to. I don't keep score. I don't have to. I've always been rich and I'll always be rich. Mom wasn't rich for a time. That's why she keeps score." Wanda leaned closer to me. "That's my theory, at least."

"It's an interesting theory," I murmured.

"She wasn't down and out poor, you know, but she

had to work for a living. I think it kind of scarred her, you know?"

Working for a living scarring someone? I nodded again, not sure how to reply.

"That's why she's dead set on fighting you for the inheritance. I guess she's afraid she'll slide back into poverty or something. Although she should know better. Stepdaddy would never let that happen to her. She'll be taken care of no matter what. Hey, don't turn here. We're another two exits away." This was said to Ron, who had taken the off-ramp.

"Shortcut," he said over his shoulder.

"Shortcut?" Wanda glared at him in the rearview mirror. "This is nowhere near our subdivision. The only shortcut through here is through the housing projects or that creepy subdivision that went belly-up. Not a safe place to be," she assured me.

Ron pulled to the side of the road and got out of the car.

"What's he doing?" Wanda demanded, reaching for the door. "Hey, wait a minute. There aren't any door handles. What is this?"

"He said it has something to do with security." Just as I spoke, Wanda's door was yanked open and someone reached in and grabbed her arm. "What's going on?"

Wanda struggled, but was pulled slowly from the car, kicking while she went with those impossibly high-heeled boots. I leaned over and tried to latch onto her other arm, but her coat slid off, landing in a puddle on the seat. "What's happening?" I struggled over the seat, aiming for the open car door while tangling with Wanda's thick coat and my own small purse, which I'd slung cross-body.

Someone thrust a gun into my face. I drew back so fast I landed half-in, half-out of the footwell. "What's going on? Who are you?"

Ron peered into the car, face framed above the gun. "Stay quiet and no one gets hurt." He slammed the door and got into the front seat. A grey-glass partition slid upward, originating from a slot somewhere ahead of me.

I kicked Wanda's coat aside and leaned forward to pound on the glass. "Stop it!" When that produced no results, I twisted to the car door, kicking at it. It refused to budge, and there was no noticeable handle for me to grab. I pressed my face against the window when the car moved forward. I spied Wanda behind me, struggling with a man who was trying to wrest her into another car. "Is this a kidnapping? Where are you taking me?" I yelled so loudly my throat hurt, but Ron didn't even flinch.

The car lurched ahead, accelerating, and I was thrown back against the seat. I fumbled at the door and the partition, but neither was movable. I pulled out my phone and flicked the display on. I began to dial 911 then I saw there were no bars. I looked at the front seat. Ron had his wrist poised over some kind of device attached to the front dash. I jammed the phone back into my bag, encountering the little good luck charm that Janice had given me. Maybe if I set off the alarm someone would hear it.

I peered outside. We were entering what appeared to be a deserted neighborhood. I tucked the little charm into my outside pocket and studied my surroundings. It reminded me of the *Back to the Future* movie where Marty McFly stood near his future home, and it looked bleak with paved roads leading to driveways that led to…nothing. In this neighborhood, there were a few houses standing, one when we passed through the gates to this wasteland and one ahead on the right. The others were in the distance, a house here and there. They all looked deserted, and all appeared worn by time and weather.

It gave me the shivers, like walking through a cemetery or past a crumbling old house. Maybe it was the standpipes poking up out of the ground, waiting for electrical or gas connections. Or maybe it was the drives, all exactly the same, all symmetrical, all spaced exactly the same apart. This had been the American Dream, every family's aspiration to have a house in the suburb that looked exactly like everybody else's house.

But this was a nightmare, not a dream. This was the suburb that people fled, this was the neighborhood of broken dreams. It was like the deserted landscape after a nuclear disaster or flood where houses were swept away, leaving only the foundations. I counted fifteen empty driveways before Ron parked the car in the driveway of a house that looked marginally in better repair than the others. The concrete front steps were cracked, and the yard was a muddy morass, but the front door appeared to be closed tightly, and the garage door didn't bow in the way others did.

Ron left the car and strode to the garage, pressing a remote he held in his hand. I pushed against the car doors, but they didn't budge. Ron disappeared into the house for a minute, then he came back out, getting into the car and pulling it into the garage. He left it running, then slid out, coming to the back and my door.

This might be my chance. I pushed Wanda's coat to the floor and leaned back on the seat, clinging hard to get a good grip. The doors clicked, and he pulled open the back door, reaching in for me.

I kicked as hard as I could, aiming for his face when he bent over. I almost got him, too, but he was fast, pivoting so most of his body was to the side, not in front of me. My foot landed on his shoulder, pushing him back. I scrambled out of the car, miraculously landing on my feet. I spun away from the vehicle and sprinted for the open garage door. I would have made it, too, but Ron got hold of my coat and hauled me back so hard my feet went out from under me, and I went down, my head hitting the concrete with a sickening thunk.

I was so stunned I just sprawled there, gasping for breath and crying from the pain. I saw feet approaching me. I tried to move, making little spasmodic motions to roll away. Then he grabbed me by the arms and pulled me upright in one fluid motion.

Pain exploded behind my eyes, the kind of sharp stabbing pain that made your stomach heave. Mine did. I leaned over and puked, noting with satisfaction that some of it hit his pants leg. The big goon rattled me like a rag doll, shaking me and dragging me to the steps into the house. "Stupid bitch," he muttered. He shook me again. I closed my eyes against the pain and the nausea.

"Oh, dear. I'm sorry I can't offer you any water to clean up. The service isn't available."

I looked up through bleary eyes. The voice came from somewhere above me. I could barely hear it through the roaring in my ears. I blinked several times, trying to clear away the tears. That's when I saw him. Bobby Reagan stood in the doorway leading to the house. "What are you doing?" I mumbled, closing my eyes again.

"Bring her inside and try not to damage her

anymore. I need her alert for what's coming."

I heard the voice from far away, moving in and out like a wave of water. I was being pulled forward, my feet dragging on pavement. Then steps were there. I was manhandled up them, someone pushing me so hard it made me gasp for breath. I let myself go and became dead weight, falling back when I lost my balance.

"Get hold of her! I want her alert!"

What the hell was he blathering about? I didn't even try to make sense of it. I focused on controlling my rebellious stomach and the agony in my head. After long moments of pushing and dragging, I was dropped onto something soft. I sniffed cautiously. The air smelled musty and stale like slightly damp carpet or mildew. I opened my eyes.

Bobby stood across the room, staring at me. "Good. You're alive." He was behind a partition, his lower body hidden. His upper half blended into the shadows, dark jacket, dark shirt. Only his round face was visible, floating in space.

I carefully moved my head one inch at a time to look around me. I was in a room next to a kitchen. I saw what I thought was a fridge and a stove and maybe a sink. I squinted and realized that the appliances were cardboard, stand-ins for the real thing. The shapes were rounded and brown and appeared to be soft. On the fridge cutout I saw what might have been pictures or maybe photographs. But they were all curled up and yellowed like small caterpillars resting on a moldy bench.

Bobby followed my gaze. "Yes, the weather has taken a toll, I'm afraid. The roof leaked and some water came in. But it's still pretty, isn't it?" He touched the pale gold laminate countertop. "It was very high-end at the time. My father sank a lot of money into this development. But he had to quit supporting it when the police arrested me. When my own brother turned me in."

"Nick," I whispered.

"It cost my father a fortune to buy off the judge and make sure my records were sealed. Then he paid another fortune when I went to prison to make sure I stayed safe there." He touched the scar on his cheek. "As safe as they could make it. But it worked out well in the long run. I made some contacts there that came in handy."

"Why are you doing this? What are you doing?" I was exhausted, bruised, and tired and overwhelmed. This was all so bizarre. "Where's Wanda? What happened to her?"

"Wanda? She's fine. Don't worry about her."

I turned my head slowly. I was sitting on a couch, and the stale smell came from it. I could feel it in my hands where they rested on the surface. It felt crumbly, the fabric old and decaying. There was no other furniture in the room. It was probably a living room. The carpet was torn in spots, exposing the wooden subfloor. The threshold between the two rooms was unfinished, the tile floor rough and uneven.

Bobby moved around the peninsula that formed a division between the kitchen and the room where I sat. Like his top half, his bottom half was in black so it was like a dark cloud moving toward me even though sunlight streamed through the windows on my right.

I gave up on studying my surroundings and focused on what he was saying, trying to put it into a context that I could understand. "What do you want with me?"

"You? I don't want you." His eyes swept over me. "I've always preferred younger women. You're far past the prime for me."

"Good. Saves me the trouble of kicking you in the balls." I squeezed my eyes shut, then opened them again. That seemed to help. The pain in my head had subsided to a dull throb, and my vision was clearing.

"You're probably more Nick's speed now. My special little brother. That's what my stepmother called him. Special. That sneaky little prick. He knew I had a girlfriend on the side. He followed me. For all I know, he watched us fuck in that garden you had."

My stomach spasmed. "What?"

"Didn't he tell you? He knew I was jumping over that wall, and I was screwing you. He never said anything because he figured you were just another of my girls. I had a lot of girls, but you were the only one I had to sneak out to see. Yeah, little Nicky was out on patrol and would check in now and then to see that his special big brother was getting laid."

My stomach spasmed harder this time. I had the horrible thought that I might throw up again. You can't barf, I told myself. They're just words. They can't hurt.

But they did.

"But on that last night he came right out and asked me about you before I left the apartment. He thought you were too young." Bobby leered at me. "You weren't too young for a good fucking now and then."

The words echoed in my head. Nick didn't just stumble on me. He knew what was happening. He knew all along what Bobby was doing.

"That's why he followed me that night. He saw me leaving there with this." Bobby tugged on the collar of his shirt but I didn't see anything. "That crazy old witch stabbed me with those scissors. Shit, I was lucky to be alive. I was bleeding like crazy. Nick went inside and got you then you know what he did? That little bastard led them to me. And because of him, I spent four years in prison." Bobby touched the scar on his face. "And that's where I got this."

Take a deep breath. Relax. It'll be okay. Deep breath. "You used me. You knew I was innocent about the world, and you used me."

"Damn right I did. And you used me." Bobby shrugged. "The stupid courts didn't see it that way. It cost my father almost everything he had to keep my records sealed and get me sent to a prison where I wouldn't be gang-raped every day by animals. My father got rid of my stepmother and started over to rebuild our lives. When I got out of prison, I helped him. I had made a few contacts there. We were able to get the capital we needed to move on."

"Got rid of your stepmother?" I croaked. "Nick's mother?"

Bobby waved a hand. "Divorced her and gave her alimony. There was no way he'd let that traitorous bitch live with us again. All his friends were laughing behind his back because they couldn't believe he'd married her in the first place." Bobby stared down at me, frowning. "I think he might have loved her. But she was lower class trash. Her and her son."

"The corny jokes at Christmastime. The Christmas crackers." I shook my head, Nick's words meshing with Bobby's from the past.

"Yeah, I told you about that, didn't I?"

I shook my head. Nick told me. Bobby didn't notice. "She was a looker, but she was low class. Once she was out of his life, my father found the kind of women he needed. There was a series of them, all working for him as his personal assistant." Bobby's eyebrows lifted and he smirked. "Yeah, they assisted all right."

"Is he still alive?"

"No, he died. In bed, with one of his women. Good way to go. I took over the business and started thinking about ways to leverage our money the best way. That's when I found Richard Bose and his family. My father always wanted me to go into politics, but I couldn't. My chance at a political career was stopped when that fucking madwoman tried to kill me, and then I was sent to prison. I couldn't take the chance that my past would be dug up. No, any political life I had was going to be behind the scenes."

Why was he telling me this? I knew, somewhere deep in my mind, that it didn't matter to him. He had been thinking about this for years, thinking about a way to get revenge. "Why didn't you just have Nick killed if you hated him so much?"

"Are you kidding? I'd be the first person they'd come after if Nick died any way other than natural causes. He was a cop, and cops take care of their own. No, I didn't see a way until you came out of the woodwork. I wasn't lying earlier. I did try to find you."

"Why? You didn't love me. Why try to find me?" He hesitated and I knew the answer. "You thought you could talk me into rescinding what I said. You thought you could convince people that I was a willing accomplice."

He shrugged. "I was young and stupid. I thought if I found you and married you, maybe it would all go away. Maybe the court would see I was sincere and just misguided. It was worth a try. I didn't really blame you.

You were young and didn't know better. But Wil Brothers did know better."

I saw a truth in his eyes, cold and emotionless. "You killed her."

"Are you kidding? Of course I didn't. I had someone else do it. I kept an eye on her all these years. When she called in Nick, I knew something was up. Then I heard about Miller and his long-lost daughter. There was a bunch of chat about that at the club and at some charity events I attended. That's when I put two and two together. The long-lost daughter was you. I got close to Richard Bose and the family. They talked about you and how you weren't interested in the money."

"You sent someone to stop me." The shadow on the shop porch, that night I went out to dinner with Nick.

"No, he was following Nick. It looked like you weren't going to jump at the chance to meet your long-lost father. So I nudged things along. I'd been wanting to settle my score with the judge anyway. This was like a two-fer. I had her killed and I got you out of your safe little home and where I could find you. I knew you'd have to come here for the funeral. But to be sure, I checked in to see if it really was you."

"But what do you hope to accomplish? What are you up to?"

"Well, my short-term objective is to get Nick here. Not too early, not too late."

"What? Nick's with his mother."

"No, he's not with her anymore. That was a false alarm, you see. By now Nick has found his bodyguard, who was disabled and left at the funeral home. He's found the note I had Wanda give you. And he knows that I have you. Nick's a smart kid. He'll figure it out."

Bobby nodded with satisfaction. "Yep, he'll figure it out, but he won't be in time. Because I'll kill you before he can find you."

Chapter 12

There were so many questions to ask I didn't know where to start. "How would Nick know I'm here?"

"I left a few clues with Wanda. Once she's found, he'll know what happened."

I focused on something I thought I could understand. "Wanda? Is she in on this?" I shook my head carefully, trying to find a position that didn't hurt.

"Wanda? That stupid idiot? Of course not. Right now the police are being diverted by searching for a kidnapped heiress. Wanda Bose. She'll be found in a few hours, blindfolded, safe, and unharmed, near a police station in one of the shabbier parts of town. The only person she saw clearly was Ron. He's on his way to Mexico right now."

"The note you gave her?" It didn't make sense. Nothing made sense. "You wrote it?"

"Of course I did. Miller had no idea his stepdaughter was going to contact you. I put the idea in her head. I think she actually loves the old bastard and wants him to be happy. So I told her I talked with him and convinced him to write a note to give to you. I had to get her and you together, you see, in order to divert attention. The police need to focus on her." Bobby glanced at his watch, an expensive-looking thing that occupied a big part of his wrist. "She should be calling home right about now, telling her mother that she's been kidnapped and is being

194

held for ransom. That will keep the police occupied. In about two hours, she'll find that her captors have left and the door isn't locked after all." Bobby smiled. "Simple."

"You can't get away with this," I said. "They'll know. It's like before. You said you'd be a suspect. Why do you think you can get away with it now?"

"Because it's been forty years. Nobody will think about me because I'll be at a fundraiser for a squeaky-clean politician. I'm one of his supporters and one of his biggest fans. I've worked hard to clean up my story."

"You're crazy."

"Why do people always say that when someone does something truly creative?" Bobby shook his head sadly. "This place has been abandoned for decades. It's owned by a shell corporation. There is nothing that ties it to me. They may not even be able to identify you. Gas explosions can be very thorough, although a bit unreliable where the timing is concerned."

"Thorough?"

"You know. Incinerating."

I struggled to speak. "I don't understand."

"It's very karmic. You and Nick ruined my life. I'll kill you. He'll know he wasn't fast enough to save you. I'll ruin his life."

"He'll kill you."

Bobby smiled faintly. "He can try. And go to prison for doing it. Where he'll die. He'll be on his way when Wanda is found. He's probably joined the search for her because she was the last person to be seen with you. Unfortunately, I can't wait. I'm going to a fundraiser. Time for me to go." He crossed the room to peer down at me. "Sorry it has to end this way." He reached out his hand to touch my face.

I leaned hard against my purse, praying the little cat figure was in the right spot.

It wasn't. Damn it all to hell. I tried shifting on the couch but my purse refused to cooperate. "Nick won't come here. Why would he?"

"Because Nick wants to be your hero. He'll show up. I have people stationed at various spots along the road. I'll be getting regular updates while I'm sipping champagne, eating hors d'oeuvres, and chatting with the high and mighty in town. Don't try to leave the house. My men have orders to shoot you on sight. Goodbye, girly." He went into the kitchen, the shadows swallowing him immediately.

I staggered to my feet and fumbled with my purse. There were voices coming from beyond the kitchen. I assumed that was the garage where I entered. I dragged out my phone and checked the display. There were still no bars. They were blocking the signal. Wasn't there some kind of emergency 911 app or something? I thought there was an override that worked even when all else failed.

A door slammed where Bobby disappeared. I caromed through the kitchen and found the door. The knob didn't turn. I whirled, making a quick check of the entire floor. Two bedrooms, one of which had obviously housed squatters or rats if the debris left behind was any indication. I almost vomited again. A bathroom that I didn't even try to enter, given the stench that came out of it. Windows boarded up in back and the windows in front partially boarded, giving only peeks of the sunset.

Okay. Don't panic. The first thing to do is get out of this house without being seen. I headed for the back where the boarded-up windows might have a gap, but I stopped.

How much time did I have? The way Bobby talked, this house might explode at any moment. But something about his phrasing told me that he was hoping Nick would be here to see it happen. Okay. The fundraiser was set to start at five o'clock. That last glimpse I had of my phone said it was four o'clock. Think. Think. Bobby said Wanda would be calling her mother now. Then in a couple of hours she'd be released. That meant six o'clock. If Nick talked to Wanda and figured it out, then maybe seven o'clock?

I had time. Some time, I amended. It felt better knowing what my deadline might be. I walked around the entire house, even hazarding a step into the disgusting bathroom. But there didn't appear any way out. There was a door leading into a basement, but I didn't have the courage to go down there in the dark.

Daylight was fast fading, too. It was almost too murky to see where I was walking. I went to the front window of the living room where the couch was and peered through the boards covering the opening. The empty street stretched out, flat and surrounded by weeds. I thought I saw movement near a house four or five driveways away from me, but I couldn't be sure. It seemed like shadows were stretching and moving everywhere.

The front door was near the window. I rattled the doorknob and to my surprise, it was loose. So loose, in fact, that I was able to get it to wobble almost out of its position. I jiggled and wiggled. Then I dug in my purse and used my lip gloss to add some moisture to the dried-out wood. I bloodied a couple of fingers and finally managed to get the entire mechanism to come free. I tugged at the door, warped with time and weather, and managed to inch it open a crack. I peeked outside.

Darkness. No streetlights and no house lights. I looked down at myself. At least I was wearing dark colors and no one would see me. Maybe. There was some light from the moon but not much. Bobby said somebody would be watching the house. Where were they? If he were planning some kind of explosion, the guards would have to be distant, right? Were they snipers or something, able to shoot from far away?

I ducked back inside and checked my phone. Holy crap, it was almost six. What about Jake and the others? Surely they were missing me by now. Damn it, Jake might have another near-heart attack when he knew I was gone. Shit. I needed to get out of here and get someplace where I could get a ride. I reached for the door and pulled it open.

Gunfire. It sounded amazingly loud in the empty neighborhood. I cowered near the door. Were they shooting at me? More gunfire. It sounded far away. There was no impact near me, so sign that I was a target. I took a chance and dashed out of the house, falling off the rotted front step and landing on my face in the muddy yard.

I barely noticed. I rolled on my side, pushed myself to my feet and began a lurching run to the next house, three driveways away. If I could hide behind it, maybe I could work my way to front of the subdivision and from there to safety.

"Get down!"

Somebody grabbed me and hauled me bodily off my feet, turning me so I was facing back the way I came. There was another gunshot, this one so close my ears burned with the noise. I struggled weakly against the arm holding me, but my headache flared up again, probably because whoever held me was firing a gun just inches away from my face.

"Are you okay?" Nick was in front of me, his hands on my shoulders as he peered into my eyes. I think that's what he said. My ears were still ringing.

I nodded but stopped when it hurt, wincing and backing away from him. He touched my head, and I slapped his hand away. "Where did you come from?"

"Come on. We can talk later." He pulled me with him, crouching and trotting through the muddy yards and over the unused driveways.

"You're early," I whispered when we paused.

"What do you mean?" He glanced at me, but immediately refocused on the street in front of us.

"Bobby said it would be a few hours. There's a bomb or something."

That got his attention. "What bomb?"

"He said there'd be a gas explosion." I tried to remember exactly what Bobby said but everything was fuzzy. "At seven o'clock. I think. He said you wouldn't figure it out because Wanda—Is she okay?"

"She's fine. She told me where they grabbed her. That's how I knew you were here."

That didn't make sense. The timing was wrong. "But you're early," I insisted.

"Talk later. Run now." He yanked me out of my crouch and dragged me, stumbling across the muddy terrain to the street. It was all I could do to stay caught up to him without falling flat on my face.

At one point he paused, raised his arm, and fired. I peered around him and saw a man drop to the ground.

"Did you kill him?"

"I doubt it. Come on."

"Do you do that a lot?"

"As little as possible. Now move!" We were off and running again, me stumbling and careening like a drunk. The only things that kept me upright were fear and Nick. We were making our way to the front of the subdivision where I could see several cars parked.

Nick suddenly stopped and dropped to his knees, dragging me with him. He put a finger to his lips, then crept forward in an odd duck-like walk, his eyes intent on the cars. That's why he didn't see the man on the left coming toward us with a raised gun. The man was near the side of a house, in the shadows.

I drew breath to yell then realized if I did that, I'd give away our location. I dug my hand in my purse and found the charm. I pressed the tummy and flung it behind me, then I lunged forward, covering Nick with my body. A shrieking alarm burst through the night, sounding like banshees from hell all screaming at one time. It was stunning, something elemental.

Nick twisted and I fell off, sprawling in the dirt next to him. He sat up and fired. This time I saw how the gun recoiled in his hand and how his arm never moved. Damn. There was more to this gun thing than I knew.

I flopped back in the dirt. Nick leaned over me. "I know," I said. "Talk later, run now." I heard footsteps running toward us and I rolled over, prepared to lunge forward and run.

"It's okay. They're with us."

I lay on my stomach, peering up at the men who approached. "Who are they?"

"Police. The good guys." Nick jumped to his feet.

"There might be a bomb or some other kind of explosive. We need to clear the area," he called.

"You're early," I said. "We should be okay for a few more minutes."

Nick put his arm around me. "Let's not wait around to see."

Twenty minutes later, I had scraped off most of the debris and was sitting in the back of an SUV. Nick was outside, talking to a group of men. All of them were wearing jeans and jackets with PPD stenciled on the back. One of the men took Nick's gun, and he was signing some papers, nodding while an older man spoke. A few minutes later he got into the car next to me, and two of the police officers got into the front seat.

"Where are we going?" I asked when the car started moving.

"We're taking you to the hospital to be checked, then I'm going with them to the Miller house." Nick nodded to the men in the front seat.

"I want to go, too. I'm fine. I don't need a hospital."

"You might have a concussion."

"I might have a fit if you try to stop me." I leaned forward. "Forget the hospital. It can wait. I want to see that son of a bitch for myself."

One of the men, a craggy-faced older guy, turned around. "You'll need to sign a waiver. We're supposed to take you to the hospital."

"Give it to me. I'll sign it."

He looked at Nick. "You were right." He turned back around and spoke in a low voice to his partner.

"Right about what?" I asked Nick.

"I said you'd want to go straight to the fundraiser."

"You bet I do. Why did they take your gun?"

"They need to investigate the shooting. It's standard procedure."

"Hmm. How did you know where to find me?"

"Wanda."

"Wanda? They found her?"

Nick laughed. "She talked her captors into letting her go. They were supposed to keep her for a few hours, but she was free after an hour. Something about a dog and a pet food foundation. You'll have to get the full story from her. When she told me where you two were separated, I knew where he'd go. That stupid subdivision was my stepfather's pride and joy."

There it was. The truth. Nick knew it the minute he said it. "I didn't know how to tell you. I wanted to apologize right away. I wanted to tell you I screwed up. But I couldn't see you because you were in the hospital. I went there, but Wil wouldn't let me in. I was a witness, and it would taint the investigation."

I nodded. That made sense.

"I was young. I didn't look up to Bobby, but my stepfather kept telling me what a great guy he was, how I should try to model myself after him. Bobby was going to do big things in the world. I don't think my mother believed him. I think she knew the truth, but she was afraid to speak it out loud."

"Your mother," I whispered. "You were afraid of what would happen to her."

He nodded. "I went to her that night, and I told her what Bobby had done. She told me to make the arrest. She knew what it would cost her, but she told me to do it anyway. She told me to do what was right." His voice trembled. "My mother lost her marriage and her home and her security because of me. Because I did what was right."

I couldn't console him. I couldn't say it wasn't his fault because it was. It was ultimately Bobby's fault, but it was also Nick's. Nick could have stopped it long before the pregnancy, long before Thell's maniacal attack.

"I couldn't stay in Rampian after that. My stepfather made sure that I wouldn't succeed in the police department. With Wil's help, I got a job in San Francisco. I made enough to support my mother and myself. Things got better after a while. Then my stepfather died, and I decided to move back here." He touched my hand. "I'm sorry. I was young and afraid. I faced a moral decision, and I failed."

"You knew what kind of man he was, and you didn't protect me." I wasn't blaming him. I was just sorting it all out.

"I was twenty years old, a new police officer, and my stepfather was the most powerful man in town. I was scared. My stepfather hated me for telling the truth. He tried to bribe me to lie. I couldn't do it. His son went to prison, and he made sure my mother and I suffered for it."

I rested my aching head back on the seat, so exhausted I was sure I'd pass out if I closed my eyes. So I didn't. I just stared at streetlights while they passed. Nick didn't pressure me to speak. He just waited, watching me. "Why did you give them my hair to test?" I finally asked.

"I did it because you have to know," Nick said.

"Who are you to—" But no. I knew who he was. He was the man who knew all about my past. He'd been there. No, he couldn't tell me what to do. But yes, he could understand why I wouldn't do it.

"I'm sorry. You're right. It wasn't up to me to make that decision for you. But if you didn't do it, you'd have to run from the knowledge for the rest of your life."

"I was prepared to do that," I whispered. "Now I can't."

"Jessa, I wanted—"

I held up my hand. "Not right now."

He fell silent. I was empty, like a shell, hollowed out. All that remained was this two-dimensional Me that was moving and talking and pretending to be cognizant. But inside I was raging and screaming and crying. If I let even a little of that out, God knows what would happen. I turned my head against the seat and stared out the window.

It appeared we were in Fancy Land now, having left the deserted suburb. This was Big Houses on impressively landscaped lots. Even in the wintertime, I could see the lines of the flowerbeds and the big trees that provided privacy. They mostly disguised the actual privacy fences around most of the estates.

Our car slowed at entry gates to a house set atop a slight hill. The driver spoke to the man at the gate, showing a badge or something in a wallet. We were ushered into the property, driving along a sedate meandering lane to a single-story house set in a grove of trees. It was a beautiful home in the Prairie style with lines and angles that made it seem to blend into the trees around it. Lights shone in tall rectangular windows, and silhouettes moved against the etched glass.

Our driver parked in front and a young man bounded toward us with a welcoming wave. "Valet service," he announced, pulling open the front door.

The driver stepped out, showed the same wallet, and the young man fell back as if pushed. "The car stays here." Without waiting to see if his order was followed, the driver joined the other man from the front seat and they strode to the front steps.

Nick and I trailed behind. I tried to scrape off some more mud from my coat but only succeeded in smearing it more firmly in place. We entered into a grand foyer and I revised my estimate of the home's size. What we saw from the front appeared modest, but apparently this house had depth. The entry area held at least thirty people, all of them moving about or standing in small groups without any visible crowding. All were dressed in formal wear, tuxedos for the men and evening gowns for the women. Jewels and baubles were highly visible, with a few tiaras here and there. Beyond the people, I saw massive double doors opened onto what appeared to be a ballroom or large hall.

The two officers with us consulted with a man in a tux holding a clipboard. I recognized an organizer when I saw one. The man looked stunned then nodded rapidly, holding up one hand in a wait-here gesture. The older officer turned to us.

"He wants to get the senator out of here before we make the arrest," he said in a low voice. "There are reporters here."

I snorted. "You're arresting one of his major backers. He's gonna get smeared no matter what he does."

"He's a politician," the other man muttered. "He'll figure out a way to spin it."

I sighed. That was probably right. A few seconds later, the organizer appeared in the doorway, nodding toward his right. We all went forward, cutting through the entryway crowd like little black rainclouds in our dirty clothes and the police with their jackets and jeans.

We'd gone just a few yards into the ballroom when the older officer stopped. He pressed a finger to his ear and nodded. The other officer did the same. He glanced over his shoulder at us. "Explosion at the Tower Heights subdivision. Two houses went up."

"Holy crap," I breathed. "Was anybody hurt?"

He shook his head and walked forward, his hand hovering near his waistband. I peeked around him and his partner and spied Bobby standing near a window with his phone in his hand. He was obviously reading a text or message of some kind. He looked confused or maybe angry.

The room was full of people holding glasses or plates, mostly in small groups around little tables. I saw Steffi Bose in the distance. She wore a dark blue evening gown with a low-cut bosom and an impressive diamond necklace that almost covered her décolletage. Her hair was upswept into a beautifully braided mass. I sniffed disdainfully. Her eyes were constantly in motion, assessing the crowd. When she glimpsed me, I thought she'd faint. Then the organizer appeared at her elbow, and she *really* looked sick.

People gave us sidelong looks when we plowed through the crowd. The officers just ignored the attention, but I took Nick's arm for support when I saw some of the baleful glares leveled at us. "The rich are different than you and I," I murmured.

"They still put on their pants one leg at a time." He squeezed my arm against his side.

"Oh my God. There she is!" The shouted words

immediately silenced all conversation in the enormous room. "Are you okay?" I was suddenly engulfed by Wanda Bose, who flung her arms around me and almost lifted me off the ground. She wore the same clothes she wore earlier in the day except she now had a jaunty tie-dyed bandana looped around her neck. "I couldn't believe it when that guy pulled the gun. O.M.G. I was so worried!" She released me then stood back to take in my appearance. "What did they do to you? Look at you! Are you okay? There's blood on your forehead."

"I'm okay." I tried to turn, but she had a grip on my arm.

"This is the lady who was kidnapped with me," she announced to everyone around us. "You just wouldn't believe what happened. We were in a car with this guy driving us and suddenly he pulls off the road and—"

The officers were almost to Bobby. He turned when Wanda yelled and saw us all coming toward him. He spun and started working his way through the crowd, which had now gathered around Wanda.

"…takes out a gun and tells me to get out of the car." Wanda pulled me closer. "We were just riding in the back seat, minding our own business, and he tells me to get out. He grabbed me. Hey. That's right. I lost my coat." She looked at me.

"It might be in Mexico," I said.

She shrugged. "I'll get another one."

I wiggled out of her grip. "I'll be right back. I need to do something." I plowed through the crowd before she could protest just in time to see Bobby making a break for one of the open patio doors. Nick was pushing aside people, and the other two officers were flat out running. I broke into a trot which turned out to be the wrong thing to do. My poor head flared into pain again, and I had to stop.

I made my way to one of the open patio doors, two or three away from where Bobby disappeared. I leaned against the frame, praying the cooler air would help ease the ache that threatened to blind me.

"You can't go anywhere," Nick called. "It's over, Bobby."

I moved away from the frame and out into the actual patio. Low lights were hung in the trees, providing some illumination. It was too cold to be out here for any length of time, but it was pleasant enough for a quick breath of fresh air. A few benches were set among low bushes. Flowerbeds lined the paths that wound through the expansive back yard.

I craned my neck to see around a topiary, looking to the left. Nick was backlit by light from the ballroom, and he was slowly walking forward. I thought I saw the other two police officers in the distance coming in through the yard behind where Nick was walking. That's when I spied Bobby. He was on a path, looking alternately at Nick and the two officers. His back was to me and he was still holding his phone. Or wait—

Damn. He was holding a gun. What the hell? How did he get into this party carrying a gun? Didn't they screen people? What was it with people and guns? I inched away from the doorway and moved into yard, keeping to the shadows cast by the house itself. Bobby was about twenty yards in front of me. Nick was to my left, moving cautiously forward. The two officers were farther away. I saw them dashing through the landscape, but it was slow going because of flowerbeds and shrubs.

"What the hell are you doing here?" Bobby

demanded. "You're supposed to be gone. You're supposed to be dead."

"At the subdivision? Wanda got away early. Your timing was off." Nick kept moving forward and that's when I remembered.

He didn't have a gun. What the hell was he doing? I glanced to my right. The two officers were getting closer but they weren't close enough. Nick was stalling him. Nick was trying to make sure the officers got there.

I sidled to my right, keeping the house behind me. Bobby was moving away, coming toward me. He was going to make a run for the house. Or maybe a run around the house, to the cars parked at the side in the valet lot. I moved again.

"We have all the evidence we need." Nick moved forward, and that made Bobby step back. I could tell he was poised to run, poised to do something crazy. His hand trembled and his whole body looked tense, like he might explode at any minute. "You'll go to prison for real this time."

Bobby turned toward him, raising his hand. "For what? You can't prove I had anything to do with her death."

"Jessa? Or Wil?" Nick asked. "Who did you kill?"

"Wil? I had nothing to do with that. And Jessa? I don't know anything about her death. That old subdivision is unsafe. Everybody knows it. I have no idea how she got there."

Hot damn. He thought I was dead. The explosion. He got word that the house exploded. He didn't know that Nick got to me in time.

"Sorry, Bobby," I called out. "You fucked up. The next time you want to kill somebody, you should make sure it gets done."

He whirled, his gun raised. Nick dove for him. I darted around a statue and was almost to them when the two officers got there. Nick had Bobby pinned to the ground, one of Nick's knees holding down Bobby's arm. The gun was off to one side.

I pushed my way past the officers and glared down at Bobby. "You son of a bitch. I'll testify against you this time, and I'll do it happily. You had Wil killed and you tried to kill me. You're going to rot in jail, you asshole." I turned, so angry I couldn't see straight.

Which is how I managed to stomp on his hand. Bobby howled but I think it was more anger than pain.

"O.M.G. I knew something was wrong with him. I knew he was a creep." Wanda Bose bounded out to me and swept me up, again, in an embrace. "I told you he was a creep, didn't I? What did he do? I'm sure we'll find out. I mean, there aren't any secrets around here, are there? Are they arresting him? Is that the Miranda thing?"

I watched the officers haul Bobby to his feet and put on handcuffs while murmuring something the entire time. "I suppose it is the Miranda thing. I don't know." I peeled myself away from her and sucked in a deep breath. "What are you doing here? I thought you were kidnapped."

"Well, when that guy grabbed me I—"

"Wait a minute." I went to Nick. "What's next?"

He touched my face. "Now we take you to the hospital. And we call Jake and tell him everything's okay. Then we sit back, have a drink, and figure out what the hell happened."

"I can have my doctor check her, you can make a

call from my study, and I'd like to have a drink with you, too, if you'll explain it all to me."

Nick and I both looked to our left. A tall man with white hair was walking toward us, one hand on a cane. He didn't look like he needed it. I thought it was more a fashion accessory than anything. He paused next to Wanda. "I want to hear about your adventures, too."

She smiled at him. "It's quite a story, Stepdaddy."

I took a step back. The man nodded. "Hello, Jessa. I'm your father."

Chapter 13

"We don't know that. There are tests to do." I leaned away, almost tripping over Nick, who stood behind me.

The man moved forward. "You look like her. You're shorter than Cindy was, but your face and your hair are hers." He stood under one of the lights from the tree. It highlighted the sculpted lines of his face. Despite his age, he was still handsome. I could see the rakish young man he had been, especially when he smiled.

His gaze went past me. "I see we've had some difficulties. Let me discuss this with the officers, and I'll join you in private. Wanda, show Jessa and Mr. Kingson to the study. And ask Dr. Mason to join us." He turned to the crowd of avidly curious people who had flocked to the patio doors. "Nothing to worry about, folks. A minor disturbance. Please, go back to the party."

Several waiters appeared on cue, gently ushering people back into the ballroom. It was amazing, really. Miller had such a presence, such a commanding way of speaking, that no one even quibbled. Everybody just meekly turned around and ignored the sight of one of their own compatriots being led away in handcuffs.

Miller joined the officers, who were moving Bobby through the garden. I started to follow him, but Wanda took my hand. "Come on. You look beat up. When Stepdaddy says to do something, it's best just to do it. He'll get his way."

I looked at Nick and he nodded. "You go with her. I'll join you in a minute." He cut through the bushes to confer with Miller and the officers.

"Damn men," I grumbled. "Leaving us out of their business."

"That's okay. Let them do the dirty work. Oh, speaking of dirty work. Hello, Mother. You remember Jessa, don't you? Your stepdaughter?" Wanda smiled prettily at Steffi Bose, who blocked our movement on the patio pavers.

"What are you doing?" Steffi hissed. "You had a guest of mine arrested?"

I stepped so close to Bose she took a step back, staring down her nose at me. "Bobby Reagan is responsible for the death of a woman I loved. I'm going to make sure he rots in prison for it, too. Right now I'm going to talk to your husband and decide if I want to participate in this fucked-up family of yours." I looked at Wanda. "Where's the study?"

"Come on. This way." She glanced at Bose. "Stepdaddy wants us there. You and Richard probably shouldn't bother us. You know what I mean. That way Richard can say he doesn't know anything about it." Wanda winked at me, then continued. "Make sure to tell Richard that I can't introduce him tonight. You'll have to do it." Wanda looped her arm through mine and tugged me to the left, toward the house. "He has a door that opens into his garden over here. Come on. We'll get a drink. I'll page Dr. Mason, too." She reached into her sweater pocket and pulled out her phone. "He's on speed dial."

"You have a doctor who lives here?"

"Sure. In the guest cottage. Stepdaddy's getting old,

so we like to have somebody on hand." Wanda put the phone to her ear and kept guiding me along a path while she talked. "Dr. Mason? It's Wanda. My stepsister is here, and she's been injured. Can you join us in Stepdaddy's study? Yes, my stepsister. Thanks."

We reached a French door, and Wanda tapped in a code on the lock. "We don't let just anybody barge in. He's very particular about his garden and his space. He'll probably give you the code later on."

I paused in the open doorway to look back at the tidy little garden, complete with a single lilac bush in the middle. "It reminds me of a garden I used to know," I whispered.

"He likes to putter around out there. Sit down." She pointed to a deep armchair upholstered in bright colorful flowers.

I sank down and sighed with relief. The chair was exactly what I needed, soft but firm, supportive but forgiving. "I'm in love with this chair."

"Everybody says that. We call it the Happy Chair." She flopped down in one that was similar but in a plain fabric. "Stepdaddy and me. Mom and Richard never come in here except to complain. So they don't usually sit down."

A knock sounded at the oversized door opposite the patio door. Wanda bounded to her feet and opened it. A small, rotund man with a shock of white hair bustled into the room, and without even being told, I knew this was the doctor. He wore pressed slacks and an immaculate white shirt and carried a small bag. "House calls?" I joked.

He regarded me with a sharp gaze. "Indeed. You appear to have had a fall. Am I right? I'm Dr. Mason.

Let's take a look." He pulled over a small chair that I think was probably designed just for that purpose, to allow him to get close without me having to move a muscle. He checked my eyes, gently felt around my scalp, had me squeeze fingers, and did a few other non-invasive checks.

"I'll clean your head wound and we'll get that bandaged, then I'll give you something for the pain. If you have any vision problems or nausea in the next few days, you go to the emergency room. Do not pause to visit a doctor, go right to emergency."

At the word *nausea* my stomach rumbled noticeably. "Sorry. I haven't eaten much today."

"We can solve that. Wanda, rustle us up some grub." I smiled at his homey language, but apparently it was commonplace because she didn't even blink. She went out of the room with an airy wave. "Now this will sting, but it's necessary." Mason fussed around my face, dabbing at cuts I didn't know I had and patting on bandages here and there.

By the time he finished, Wanda had returned with a plate of appetizers, bottles of water, and a bowl of potato chips and two kinds of dip. "I love chips and dip," she confessed, setting all the food on a table between the two chairs.

"I hope we're planning on something more than water." The door to the garden opened, and August Miller and Nick came into the room. "Is it okay for the patient?"

Mason bundled his bandages and bottles into the small bag. "A small bit of brandy might be in order." He handed me a twist of paper. "Here are two super OTC pain relievers. Take one now and one at bedtime with another brandy. And don't forget what I said. If you have any problems, you go straight to the emergency room and demand to have an X-ray."

"I'll make sure she does," Nick said.

Miller's sharp gaze went from me to Nick then back to me. "I'm glad to know someone will be monitoring your health. Thank you, Dr. Mason."

"Just call if you need me." The doctor gave Wanda a friendly tap on the shoulder, then left. When he opened the door, I heard the murmur of voices, but when it closed, the room was silent again. Great soundproofing, I thought.

Miller smiled at Wanda, who was in her chair, a container of dip in hand. "I'm pleased you're none the worse for your adventure." He sat down behind the desk in an enormous office chair with a well-worn leather seat and arms. "Mr. Kingson, the brandy is behind you, in the cabinet next to Jimi Hendrix. I believe Wanda would prefer a beer. It's underneath, in a small fridge."

I turned in my chair. "Damn. That is Jimi." It was the Independence Hall poster dated 1968, framed and— I squinted. "Is that signed?"

Miller nodded. "It was hard to lose him so young. He and Janis were the initial members of the 27 Club."

"The 27 Club?" I asked.

"Rock musicians who died when they were 27," Nick said behind me. "Kurt Cobain, Janis Joplin, Jimi Hendrix, Jim Morrison."

"Amy Winehouse," Wanda added. "Thanks." She took the beer Nick handed her.

"To lose so many so young." Miller's eyes were fixed on a picture on the corner of his desk. I couldn't see it completely, but it appeared to be a woman with pale hair. "Thank you." He took the glass Nick handed him. "Now can someone fill me in on what has been going on?"

"Forty years ago I screwed up." Nick's voice was immediately behind me.

I peered up at him over the back of the chair. "You did what you thought was right at the time. It just wasn't the best thing for me."

Wanda handed me a paper plate that held shrimp, cheeses on crackers, and what looked like a tiny sandwich. "Well, four hours ago I was kidnapped," she said.

Miller nodded. "I can't wait to hear about it, but let's get some background information first. Mr. Kingson, perhaps you can summarize."

Nick handed me a glass then settled into a chair near the patio door, a beer in his hand. "Bobby Reagan raped Jessa when she was a teenager, and I testified against him at his trial. I was a young police officer at the time. His father paid off the system, so Bobby only had to serve a minimal sentence. Jessa went into hiding, aided by Jake and Wil Brothers. They helped her acclimate to a new life because she'd been sequestered for seventeen years and had no knowledge of the world."

Wanda listened to this with wide-eyed astonishment, shoveling chips and dip into her mouth with methodical precision. "You were like a nun?" she breathed.

"Sort of."

"Wow. I always knew he was creepy. What a motherfucker." Wanda's gaze swung to her stepfather. "Sorry. I know you hate it when I use bad language."

"In this case, it's justified." Miller was resting back

in his chair, partially in shadow because of the low lighting in the room. "Jessa, I'm responsible for setting you on that path. I gave you up for adoption when you were a baby."

"We don't know that for sure," I began. "The testing has to be done."

Miller shook his head. "You're my daughter. I'm certain of it. I trust Jake Brothers and I trust Nick Kingson, and they said you're the girl in the tower." He leaned forward, clasping his hand on the desk blotter, the light illuminating his face. "I did search for you. We couldn't take care of a child. We were young and reckless and stupid. Cindy fell into a depression, and I didn't know what to do. She self-medicated and got hooked. I was afraid she'd die without the drugs. We thought an adoption was the best thing for you."

He drew in a long, shuddering breath. "It wasn't enough to save her. I tried to get her into treatment, but it was too late." When he raised his face, his eyes glistened with tears. "After Cindy died, I wanted to find you." He broke off, staring at the photo, memories strong in his eyes. "I wanted a part of her. When I went back to find you, the woman told me you'd been adopted and there was nothing to be done. It was a private adoption and the couple who had you did not want to be contacted."

He sighed heavily, his handsome face twisted with grief. "You were there the whole time. You were just a few miles away. If I had known." He closed his eyes briefly. "I went back to Europe. I didn't want to stay here. I didn't want to be reminded of what I lost. I consoled myself with the thought that you were living a typical American life. I celebrated each of your birthdays and imagined what you looked like, what you were doing. Did you join the Girl Scouts? Were you a cheerleader? Were you in the Honor Club? Did you play sports? Were you dating? Were you going to college?"

I smiled faintly. "None of those things."

"I am so sorry for what you went through. Please believe me. If I had known, I would have moved heaven and earth to bring you out of there. She was so convincing. She had paperwork and pictures."

"It's all right," I said softly. "No, my life wasn't normal, but it was the only life I knew. I never missed anything because I didn't know there was anything to miss. I didn't know about high school and cheerleading and sororities and sports." I looked to my right, to Nick. "I survived and it's made me who I am today. I don't blame you."

He met my gaze and nodded, swallowing convulsively. He knew what I was saying. There was blame enough to go around between my parents, Thell, Bobby, Nick, and even myself. I could have chosen not to let Bobby into the garden that day. I could have told Thell about him, but I didn't until it was too late. I knew it was wrong to lie to her, but I did. We were all to blame for what happened to me.

Miller—my father—leaned back. "Now that I've found you, I'm going to see to it that you're included in the decisions about my estate." He glanced at Wanda with a bemused smile. "Both of my daughters will be included. We'll do it sooner rather than later. It appears I'm obligated to set up a foundation, am I right?"

"Shall I tell my story now?" Wanda asked. "I mean, old history is good and all that, but this just happened, and it's important."

"By all means. Tell us." My father steepled his fingers in front of him and watched her, his eyes occasionally going to me to gauge my reaction.

"Okay, well. Jessa and I were in a car. There weren't any door handles inside, which I thought was weird, but the guy driving said it was okay, so whatever. We were coming here to see you, Stepdaddy, because Jessa read your note and she wanted to talk to you."

"Bobby Reagan wrote the note," I interrupted. "Your stepfather had no idea you were working to get us together."

Wanda's next potato chip paused halfway to her mouth. "That little jerk. You mean he planned all this? It wasn't a real kidnapping?"

I nodded.

She breathed out a long sigh. "That mother—" She jammed the chip in her mouth and mumbled something.

"Tell us what happened," I prodded. "After he grabbed me, he was going to—" I glanced at Miller, and he shook his head. "—was going to hurt me. He said you'd be held for hours and that Nick wouldn't be able to find me until you were released."

"That asshole. Well, about that." Wanda took a long slug of beer and belched. "Sorry. Okay, so this guy grabs me out of the car, and he put this face mask thing over my head. It stunk, like old socks or something." She made an amazingly ugly face. "Somebody tied up my hands behind my back, and I was tossed into this car. It stunk, too. Like wet dog. But there's a reason for that. I'll explain in a minute."

"Good," I murmured, nibbling at the food on the plate.

"Okay, so, somebody is driving this car. I was

yelling and kicking the seat and trying to get out, but he kept driving, and I was afraid if I fell out of the car, I'd, like, end up in the middle of traffic, so I was careful to just try to kick at whoever was driving. I hit the dog once, I think. Because I heard a little yip."

"A dog?"

"I'll get to that. Okay, so, we're driving, and we get to this place. It's like a little shack kind of place made out of cardboard. Well, not all cardboard but it's like there was a house, and the holes and things got patched with cardboard."

"I thought you were wearing a mask or something?" Nick asked.

"It was holey. I could peek through in spots. It really did stink. I had to wash my face several times to get the smell off." Wanda looked down at the dip container she held and apparently decided she'd had enough of that. She picked up the other container and scooped out a huge amount with a chip.

"So we're in this place and I hear the dog. It was all whiney. I asked what was wrong and the guy said his dog was hungry. And I said, well, feed him then. And the guy started telling me how he didn't have any money, and the only reason he agreed to help the *cabrone*—I think that's what he said—was because he had to get money to buy food for himself and his dog." Wanda munched a chip reflectively.

"Well, I know money. I mean, let's face it. So I said, Hey, I'll give you a thousand dollars right now if you just drive me back to where you found me. I won't call the cops, I won't rat you out, I'll just give you the money."

"How were you going to get him the money?" Nick asked.

"I'm getting to that. Heck, I told him if he took me to a pet store, I'd buy him all the dog food he needed. I have a credit card. I could buy out the store. He wasn't sure about that, but I could tell he wasn't crazy or anything. He was just worried."

Wanda looked at us for confirmation. I nodded slowly.

She continued. "Okay, so, we started talking, and it turns out his dog hasn't been to a vet in a long time because he's homeless—the guy, not the dog. Well, the dog, too, because he lives with the guy, whose name is Juan, by the way. Juan was worried about the dog's teeth. And, well, think about it. If the dog has bad teeth, Juan probably does, too, and how do you eat kibble with bad teeth? The dog, not Juan. But he can't take the dog to a vet because, you know, money. So I said, well, there are mobile vets, aren't there? Can't they come here, wherever here is, and help the dog?"

She paused and looked at each of us in turn. "Well, right?"

I could only nod dumbly.

"So we keep talking, and it turns out he's from Honduras and I said, well, hey, our cook is from Honduras, maybe you know her, but he didn't know her, but we talk for a while, and it doesn't sound like he's a bad guy. He just had some bad luck. He lost his job and didn't have money, so he tried to steal some dog food and the police got him and he was supposed to pay a fine, but how could he? He didn't have any money."

Nick and I exchanged a look. "She's a force of nature," he murmured.

Wanda smiled, taking that as a compliment. "He managed to scrape together enough to pay the fine, but then he lost his apartment, and he had to live in that cardboard house with a bunch of other people who were gone right then because they were out going through trash cans, looking for food. Yuck. And a lot of folks he knows have had bad luck and some of them have pets and they can't take care of the pets the way they should."

Wanda glanced at her father. "That's where you come in. I said, well, hey, maybe my stepdaddy can set up some kind of pet food foundation thing where homeless people can get vet help and food for their pets. Because homeless people love their pets, too. He got really excited by that idea and, well, long story short, we need to set that up because I told him if he let me go, I'd get it done." She beamed at Miller. "Okay?"

I looked at Nick. His eyes were wide with astonishment. "He just let you go?" Nick asked.

"Oh, no, of course not. I mean, yes, he drove me back to where we were, but I told him he could come here tomorrow and I'd give him the money and we'd talk about the foundation. So make sure when he comes here, he's allowed in the gate. I'd better talk to the front guards about that." Wanda bobbed to her feet.

"I'll handle it," Miller said. "Sit down and finish your story."

"Oh, yeah. So we drive back to the place, and I finally get to meet his dog. I didn't take off the ski mask thing. It was one of those knit hats, so that's why it smelled so bad. But we get to the place, and I open the car door and get out and his dog gets out. Juan said I could pet him so I pulled up the mask thing a bit and it was the most adorable dog. A labra-something. So wiggly and cute. Not purebred, but cute. Who knew? Well, that's true. Janie Simpson has a half-breed dog but it's more drooly than cute. I had no idea homeless people had pets. I think we should do something, Stepdaddy."

"We will, dear. Perhaps you can go see the gate guards now and make sure your friend is allowed in tomorrow." Miller watched her jump to her feet. "Wanda? Where did you get the neckerchief?"

She touched the brightly hued bandana. "Juan gave it to me. I gave him my watch because he didn't think I'd keep my promise, so I gave him my Rolex and told him to bring it tomorrow and he gave me this scarf thing." She looked at Nick. "That's what I meant about the money. I just gave him my watch. The scarf is pretty, isn't it?" She flung open the door and left, slamming it behind her.

I leaned back in my chair, exhausted.

"I wonder if she even knew she was in danger," Nick said.

"Oh, she knew," Miller said. "Wanda is an intelligent woman and an astute judge of people. I have no doubt that she correctly assessed her captor as a man at the end of his rope, and she recognized the love he had for his pet. Wanda can work almost any situation to her advantage."

"She seems like a ditz," Nick muttered.

"Looks can be deceiving." Miller's voice was decidedly sharp. He regarded me. "You're tired and in pain. I meant what I said. I do want your input on how to handle my estate. I don't think there's any reason to wait until I'm dead to do it, either."

"Really?"

He nodded. "My wife's protests to the contrary, I am not senile nor am I insane. I simply want to make sure your mother's estate is handled the way she'd want it to be. That money has nothing to do with my second wife."

"She doesn't see it that way," Nick commented.

"Steffi and I have an understanding. Now that I've found my daughter, I'll make sure she complies." Miller smiled faintly, but I saw a hint of ice in his blue eyes. "How do you feel about it?" he asked me.

"I'd like some time to think about all this. Things have been thrown at me so fast that I don't quite understand what I feel." I didn't dare look at Nick when I said it because he was one of those *things*. "Give me a few months to consider everything."

"I understand. A lot has happened." Miller came around the desk to stand in front of me and I stood. "Thank you for coming here and letting me see you."

It seemed the most natural thing in the world to go into his arms for a hug. My father.

****

I stayed with Jake for a week before returning to Iowa. Nick was in and out of the house, but we had no opportunity to be alone together. I was glad of it. I still had too many answers, and I didn't know what to feel about it all.

Jake came to Iowa for Christmas, then I settled back into my routine. I was in regular communication with my father, who was an adept Zoom user. Wanda peppered me with questions via FaceTime at least four or five times a week. She was busy with the Furry Food Friends Foundation and appeared to be enjoying herself doing it.

It was mid-April when I was told I needed to return to Rampian to prepare for Bobby's trial. It would be held in Portland in order to gather a wider jury pool. I had to give official depositions and be available for questioning and subsequent testimony.

I was sitting at my desk in the store when I heard the front bell ring. "Can I help you?" Janice asked.

"What a marvelous little store! What is that, a wild cat or a lion?"

I recognized that enthusiastic voice.

"It's a bobcat. The Fighting Bobcats. It's our school mascot," Janice answered, her voice with a hint of incredulity.

"It's adorable. I want one. Ooh, look at that. What is it?"

"It's a tea cozy. You put the pot here and the cup here."

"I want that, too. I don't drink tea, but maybe I'll meet somebody who does. I love the fabric. Those puppies are too cute. Where's Jessa?"

There was a pause. "I beg your pardon?"

"Jessa. She's around here, isn't she? Jessa? Where are you?" Wanda's voice echoed in the shop, bouncing off the Fighting Bobcat stuffed animals, the recycled fabric handbags, and the crocheted potholders.

"I'm back here, Wanda," I called.

"Oh, look at that. What a clever idea. I would never have thought to use old blue jeans for a purse. I think I need that. Oh, and this one. Look at it. The perfect size for my phone. Where are you—Oh, look. I haven't seen one of these in years. It's a vinyl record, and look what they did with it." Suddenly she was at my door, peering inside. "You have the most interesting things in this store."

Janice was behind her, looking thoroughly confused, her arms full of items which Wanda had apparently plucked off the shelves. "This lady is here to see you," she said.

Wanda flounced into my office and dropped into a chair. She wore faded jeans, a flannel shirt, and sneakers. She had apparently dressed for her idea of "farm country," although I suspect the jeans were Calvin Klein, the shirt was Gucci, and the shoes were custom-made Converse.

"I found you," she said happily, shrugging out of her nylon jacket. "This store is adorable, but you need a cat."

"I've told her that," Janice said, sidling into the office and taking the other chair.

"Absolutely. A cat. One that's fat and yellow. Maybe get one of those tabby ones, too. I've met some tabby cats at Furry Food and they're usually pretty mellow. Stepdaddy sent me to bring you home. We need your help with Furry Food."

"Furry Food?" Janice wrinkled her nose. "Who wants furry food?"

"It's food for the pets of homeless people. We're calling it the Furry Food Foundation."

"No, you should call it the Food for Furry Friends Foundation." Janice counted on her fingers, juggling a tea cozy, two denim bags, a vinyl record book stand, and a Fighting Bobcat sweatshirt. "The 5F fund."

"Oh, I like that. Hi, I'm Wanda Bose."

Janice nodded. "I guessed. She told me about you."

"Juan is doing the best he can, but we need help."

"Who's Juan?" Janice asked.

"He's the guy who kidnapped me. Like I said, he's doing a good job, but we need some help, and Stepdaddy said, go get Jessa. She has to come here anyway, so let's make sure she knows she'll have to stay to get us on track." Wanda beamed at me. "So here I am."

"You hired the guy who kidnapped you?" Janice

asked.

Wanda's head bobbed. Her hair was piled up in a messy bun, and wisps danced around her face. "He's in charge of outreach. But we need help with the day-to-day. Stepdaddy thought, well, Jessa manages a store, so maybe you can help us get that going. I can't do it because I'm working on that campaign of his to help drug addicts. Did you know that many BIPOC children are born into families with drug problems? That means Black, Indigenous, and People of Color," she added.

Janice nodded, eyes wide at this onslaught.

"It's all because of poverty, of course. That's the root cause. I'm taking classes about it."

"About poverty?" Janice asked.

"No, about social work. You need to come home, Jessa. Nick needs you."

"What?"

"Who?" Janice demanded. "Nick? The guy who was here last year?"

"Nick Kingson. I've talked to him a lot because I wanted his ideas for Furry Food, and he's an ex-cop, so he knows about addictions, too. He's moping around, Jessa. He misses you. He's out at that stupid cabin of his and just mucking around. He painted it a horrible brown color. It's just terrible," she confided to Janice. "I took a picture. It looks like turds."

Janice burst out laughing. "Turds?"

"You know, all brown and icky looking. That place needs a woman's touch. He has a firing range there. Did you know that? For guns and things. And I went inside and, well…" Wanda glanced back at the store. "He could use a few things from here to brighten that place up. Jake said he's moping."

"You're in touch with Jake?" He had never told me any of this during any of our weekly phone conversations.

"Sure. He and Stepdaddy have become friends. Jake comes over for dinner now and then. He likes the Happy Chair, too. Jake and his wife helped Jessa after she was rescued," Wanda informed Janice.

"Yeah, I knew."

"His wife was murdered by a low-life asshole hired by Bobby Reagan. Not Juan. He was just hired to kidnap me. He only did it because he needed the money. So you'll come home, right? And help us all?"

I leaned back in my chair. "Well, sure, I'll do what I can and—"

"Good. We flew into the airport in Des Moines. It's the nearest place that could handle our jet. Let's get packed and go."

"What?"

"What?" Janice and I spoke simultaneously.

"I brought the company jet. I'm sure you can manage things while she's gone, right?" Wanda asked Janice.

"Well, sure I can."

"Look, I can't just drop everything and go." I saw Janice's incredulous look and changed tactics. "I can't just barge in on Nick. It was a fling. You know, just a fling."

Both Wanda and Janice shook their heads. "Honey, I've known some flings in my day, and he is not a fling. He is a Thing. He is the Real Thing with a capital R and a capital T." Janice glared at me. "Do not pass up the Real Thing."

"What she said." Wanda jerked a thumb at Janice.

"But I—" But what? I stood, my heart pounding so fast I thought I might pass out. What was I waiting for? An engraved invitation?

"Let me ring these up. Oh, and I want to show you the pet section. We might find some things for those furry friends."

I stood there, staring at the doorway after Janice and Wanda left. Nick knew about my past. Nick had been there for me. Nick knew…

Nick knew me.

"…fabulous! Can the person who makes these make a couple hundred of them? I want our Furry logo on it and I'll give one to everybody who…"

I smiled. It was time to go home.

****

Two days later I drove down a back country road, making a left turn onto a graveled lane. A few seconds later, the small cabin came into view. Wanda was right. The color was all wrong. Maybe not turd-like, but definitely not pleasant.

I parked near the front porch and surveyed the building. It appeared solid but, well, rustic. Two windows on either side of the front door and the beginnings of a yard to one side with some scraggly grass. A parking area on the other side where a truck sat.

I stepped onto the porch and raised my hand to knock.

"I wasn't sure if I'd see you again. Are you back here for the trial?"

I turned. Nick walked to me from the grove of trees that hid the house from the road. He wore old, baggy jeans, a paint-stained sweatshirt and heavy work boots. I looked beyond him. "Wanda said you have a practice range."

"Yeah, she wants me to teach her how to shoot a shotgun."

"A shotgun? Why does she want to learn to handle a shotgun?" I stepped off the porch and met him in the drive.

"She assured me she doesn't plan to kill anything, but she figured if an intruder saw her with a shotgun, he'd run in the other direction. I told her she was probably right."

I was just a foot away from him now. "I wasn't sure you wanted to see me. Then I decided I didn't care if you did or not. I wanted to see you." He was staring at me so intently I felt like a deer in the headlights.

When he was next to me, I realized I was holding my breath. He didn't speak, so I said lightly, "I heard you might need a woman's touch around here." I looked over my shoulder at the house.

He looked down at me, then slowly smiled, a smile I felt all the way to my toes. "Sure. Touch anything you want."

I raised my hand and splayed my fingers over his chest, above his heart. "Thanks. I think I will."

A word about the author...

J L Wilson writes mysteries, reincarnation romances, time-travel novels, and dystopian books. Check out her website at jayellwilson.com or her book list at https://bit.ly/JLWbooks.